Defying Destiny
Eighteen Inspiring Icons of Pune

Prof. (Col) N. Ram Gopal

VISHWAKARMA
PUBLICATIONS
VP

Defying Destiny - Eighteen Inspiring Icons of Pune

Edition - July 2016
© Author
rgopal44@yahoo.com

ISBN - 978-93-85665-18-9

Published by:
Vishwakarma Publications
283, Budhawar Peth, Near City Post,
Pune- 411 002.
Phone No: (020) 20261157
Email: info@vpindia.co.in
Website: www.vpindia.co.in

Cover Design Consultant
Arnav Taode
Cover Sketch of Shaniwar Wada Fort
Soumya Iyer

Typeset and Layout
Gold Fish Graphics, Pune.

Readers Praise

Col Ramgopal's rendition of lives well lived should be a great source of inspiration to all. The profound messages articulated in a pointed manner in the nuanced narrative is the work of a very empathetic teacher who connected at a very deep level with his students. Each story brings home the universal message that there is no stopping anyone, if only one dared to try"

Sastabhavan Kutty,
Head - Strategic Projects, Tata Motors Pune

A gripping narrative of some 18 common men's uncommon stories... to put it in Prof (Col) N Ram Gopal's words, their enthusiasm to live and the enthusiasm to share, their ability to rise from nowhere, move along the growth path, explore life Beyond Horizons and become icons in their respective fields. Defying Destiny has been a "pleasurable adventure" for the author to explore the world of biographical short stories. And in the process, he has taken the readers along a journey towards a life that offers alternatives and next opportunities, particularly for those "who never give up". An inspiring read.

Saumyadipta Chatterjee
Assistant Editor Times of India Pune

Now, more than ever, it is important that we talk about real heroes, whose superpowers were integrity, hard work and determination. This is a chronicle of the lives of 18 Punekars, each a nation builder in their own right, simply narrated, these legacies will continue to inspire and change lives. A must read, so we can remember to make the right choice when the time comes.

Karuna M John
Journalist & Media, Information and Communication Consultant

It's easy to read, has fast paced narration and is visual in description. The stories are gripping, inspiring and thought provoking. Loved it and I am sure it's going to inspire at least some short story tellers around.

Anupama Mallajosyula
Sub-Editor: New Indian Express

Defying Destiny is an excellent collection of autobiographical real life stories. The author has done a commendable job in terms of selecting the iconic personalities and interacting to gain an insight into their lives, and finally reducing the real life stories into short, interesting and highly readable compositions. The human personal qualities that are highlighted are so fundamental in nature that every reader would benefit by imbibing them. These qualities add up to make a good human being, an achiever and most importantly a good citizen. Well done Ram.. Look forward to more such books.

Major General Chandra Prakash (Retd) Former Additional
Director General, NCC, New Delhi

Each of the stories gives an in-depth account of the accomplishments of the great Punekars. What is worth mention in the biographies is that unlike any typical biography, it does not dwell too much into the historical background but focuses more on the important milestones of their lives. The simple language used and easy writing make it a pleasure to read. Having read these stories, I feel even more proud to call myself a fellow Punekar.

Manojit Acharya
Managing Director, Jungheinrich Lift Truck India Pvt Ltd

A very well written, easy read book which explores beyond the hurdles of life. I like the expression and the effective way each story has been expressed. Key learning's aptly summarize the essence of each story without being condescending thus reinforcing those qualities that one needs to acquire. A very good read.

Meenal Thakur
Reporter: Mint

"The first thing which made me indulged into reading these stories is the writing style. The choice of words is so apt as they juxtapose at the same time humbleness and achievement without hyperbole. It seems as though no other words would express better. I knew each person from the story, but I knew only about their success and good work but not the real lives they lived. Prof Ram Gopal introduces the real person in each one of them in such a wonderful way that it makes the book truly worth a read."

Pournima Patil
HR Professional

Being a part of this book has been the biggest fortune for me. Unlike other books, it covers real time inspirational stories of the real life legends. Each story gives a unique lesson for life bringing home a message that could be a catalyst for change."

Nikita Guru
Market Research Associate Markets & Markets

It might seem "greedy" for some, but for me whenever I read anything what matters most is what I get from it; be it knowledge or sheer entertainment. This book is an excellent amalgamation of knowledge and simplicity coupled with the " Story Telling" approach of Col Ramgopal, thus making it unique and one of its kind. The entire narrative is so beautifully crafted that you feel that you are living along with the person. Sometimes, the writer has strategically used dialogue format for making it more personal. At first, I felt this is a collection of biographies; after reading, I realized that it's not about person's success but about the way that person became successful. It is not just a life story but a journey through their own eyes and using Col Ramgopal's spectacles as filter.   It is a must read for all who think there is nothing to get inspired!

Amey Surendra Pangarkar
Marathi Play Writer

The stories in this book serve a reminder to everyone that things happen in life for a reason; it is for one to be patient enough to find that reason. Frustrations of life, big and small, pave the way to better things... an important lesson to be learnt at every stage of life. The power of conviction and sincerity in one's work, play an important role in shaping one's life. It is important for each individual to realise his or or her self worth and prove the same to the world.

Prof Pallavi Murdeshwar IBS Business School Pune

INDEX

Foreword

Robin Banerjee
CEO & MD
Caprihans India Ltd, Mumbai, India

The book you are holding is a marvellous portrayal of eighteen real-life achievements of extreme grit and determination, fighting all odds to make lasting contributions filled with amazing, fresh insights. It's all about real world, people with blood and sweat, running their adrenal to achieve the unachievable.

Chandu Borde, donned the Indian colors between 1958 and 1970. Playing against the mighty fast bowlers of West Indies in the 1958 series, he froze in front of their fiery bowling spells failing miserably, only to make a great comeback in the fourth match. None of the setbacks ever led Borde to take a step back.

Wires, cables and pipes in India are synonymous with Finolex. It is the rags to riches story of the little boy Prahalad Chabria migrating from Pakistan, having no formal education, ultimately creating one of the finest organizations fashioned on trust and integrity.

From the refugee camp in Lonavla to taking over as the first lady CEO of a multinational engineering company Alfa Laval, Leela Poonawalla set an unprecedented precedent in the annals of India's corporate history. An astounding story of confidence and self-motivation.

A little boy who grew up studying under the street lights, ultimately shaped the destiny of India's science and technology, was none other than India's perhaps most famous scientist of recent era - Dr. Raghunath Mashelkar. His inspirational story keeps us spell bound.

An outstanding example of first generation success in building an iconic educational institution in Pune has been depicted by

Dr. Viswanath Karad. A person despite difficulties, created the first private engineering college in Maharashtra. MIT's success story in the world of education through Karad's dedication is epical.

DSK Toyota screams out of numerous hoardings and name plates in Pune. D S Kulkarni, built several businesses from a scratch. His message embraces the value of dignity of work.

Children with down-syndrome have an arduous journey in life. Being differently abled, they are rarely accepted by the society as 'normal'. Gauri Gadgil's experience was no different. But she fought all odds to become the champion swimmer of India.

Pandit Suresh Talwalkar is a tabla magician. His Gurukul is simple, spartan and symbolic. A strong believer of guru-sishya relationship which he says is the harbinger for learning music.

Abhijit Pawar has been instrumental in giving Sakal a new identity different from its pre-independence era to a modern look. His philosophy has been to resist sensationalism & focus on sensitization.

One of the best conversationist Maharashtra has ever produced is Sudhir Gadgil. From Indira Gandhi to Lata Mangeskar; from Bal Thackrey to Madhuri Dixit, Sudhir has interviewed the who's who of India.

Not many would give up cushy jobs in the USA to fulfill dreams of nation building. Dr. Anand Deshpande precisely did that in his persistence to create one of the finest Indian software company – Persistent, a company with a focus on society.

Rags to riches stories are many, but how many instances have you heard of giving up riches to help the rag bearers? Shantilal Mutha, once a successful real-estate baron sacrificed prosperity at the altar of social upliftment.

Who has not heard or watched Dr. Shriram Lagoo, the brilliant actor His story is a reminder that it's never late to pursue passion. His love for stage drove him make a choice many may find impossible to make.

Can you believe that an engineer can be an exponent of Ayurveda and spiritual healing? Dr Balaji Tambe says that his arrival to the world is for fulfilling preordained duties to heal people's lives.

Superman created the India's first super-computer – Dr Vijay Bhatkar. You may also be surprised to know that he was also responsible for bringing colour TV transmissions to our homes. When USA refused the technology to manufacture super computers, it was Dr Bhatkar, the father of India's super-computer gave India the place of pride.

Chatrapathi Shivaji, the 17th century founder of the Maratha Empire, is revered in Maharashtra. Little is known of the one behind making Shivaji the legend more legendary amongst the common man. He is Babasaheb Purandare. An avid historian and a passionate patriot.

If you pass through Pune city, you are sure to encounter one of the best three orthopaedic hospitals in India. Its promoter Dr Kantilal Sancheti, a slow learner in studies, became to be one of the best known doctor - a story of sheer guts and grit.

Pune symbolises education, and one such hub is the Symbiosis group. Dr Shantaram Mujumdar's journey to create this iconic institution, in spite of repeated hurdles is unique. An example of persistence and commitment.

An exact formula for success has never been defined. But the closest thing we can do is to follow the ones who have been successful and perhaps learn a lesson or two to make our lives more meaningful, successful and above all, happy. The eighteen short stories of Pune-legends are an honest attempt to do so. Simply told, lucidly written and more importantly short and sweet.

Author's Preamble

Defying Destiny - Eighteen Inspiring Icons of Pune was conceived to show case ordinary individuals who have emerged to be extraordinary. Positivity, sheer determination and a passionate desire to make a difference spurred them to redefine success. Their life stories highlight one fact; that success is not about power, elevation to a position or affluence. It is more about excellence, empowerment and adding value to the lives of people they influenced. These stories are intended to reaffirm that goodness of intention backed by goodness of actions will ultimately result in larger good to all.

The most common thing about people who stand above the rest is that they think, act and conduct themselves in an uncommon manner. This exceptional attribute is characterized by many qualities. They believe in themselves, remain undaunted by difficulties and challenges, their focus is steadfast and unwavering, they engineer solutions from the problems they encounter, retain a strong sense of character in difficult times, develop keen understanding of human nature, observe, assimilate and acquire inputs from the environment, demonstrate keenness for continuous learning through unlearning and remain open to change.

The purpose of this venture is to sensitize young minds with life stories of people who struggled and succeeded in spite of limitations. To prove to young readers "that success is more of mind and thinking beyond circumstances". Each of these stories validate one significant message "That life offers alternatives and there will always be a "Next Opportunity" for those who never give up".

To reinforce the lessons from each of these stories, Key Learning Values have been summarized and extracted at the end of each story. I do hope, readers will find the stories inspiring and invigorating, leaving an imprint somewhere on their minds to be retrieved in times of challenge; giving them courage, confidence and conviction to face and surmount the hurdles.

The process of undertaking this most pleasurable adventure of writing biographical short stories on each of the chosen personalities has been an experience beyond words. Interacting with each one of them, from various fields of expertise has shown one thing that is common; the enthusiasm to live and the enthusiasm to share and unbridled energy to go on without respite.

I would like to express my gratitude to each of the 18 Icons who willingly and enthusiastically shared their life story. I am deeply impressed with their gracious conduct, simplicity and humility. Their unstinted support and revelations made the entire exercise of undertaking this venture, an intellectually stimulating expedition.

- Prof. (Col) N. Ram Gopal

Acknowledgements

Accomplishments, however big or small are never an outcome of individual effort. A lot of advice, support, guidance, brainstorming and time is spent by others whose contributions need to be acknowledged with humility.

At the outset, I am deeply indebted to Col. N. S. Nyayapati, (Retd.) Founder of Care India Medical Society, for acceding to my request to accept the royalty from the sale of this book towards treatment for cancer affected children from underprivileged society to augment their outstanding work.

My grateful acknowledgement to Rotary Club of Pune East, for its unstinted support in the form of ideation and facilitation. Though many have played their part, I would like to mention Mr. Pritam Bhatevera, for his impeccable support in enabling the appointments, meetings and administrative support. Mr. Shital Shah for his constant motivation and Mr. Srinivas Kendale for initiating the idea of writing this book.

I am truly obliged to Mr. Robin Banerjee, CEO & MD, Caprihans India Ltd, for his erudite foreword.

The cover credits are indeed an effort symbolizing commitment. Nothing can express adequately to acknowledge the effort of Soumya Iyer for the outstanding sketch that adorns the cover and the pleasing design created by Arnav Taode, who spontaneously joined from New Zealand.

My students Amey Pangarkar & Nikita Guru for editorial assistance and review .

Mr Bhujbal and his team for the exceptional video support which enabled me to compile the stories effectively.

Lastly, my better half Anubha for her incisive advice in shaping the story lines and insisting many a times, accept a view point which invariably was better than mine. A very special mention for my son Anurag & daughter Akanksha for their critical evaluation.

Not to forget the most important of all Mrs. Scharada Dubey & Mr. Vishal Soni of Vishwakarma Publications and for their strong commitment in making this book a reality.

My grateful acknowledgements to all the eighteen iconic personalities whose life, contribution and character has been inspiring and will continue to inspire.

Ram Gopal

This Book is Dedicated to My Parents
Shri. N. K. Acharya and Late Dr. M. Sowbhagyavalli
Whose Life by Example Exemplified
"Simplicity, Honesty, Virtue and Values"

C. G. Borde

In life every opportunity must be seized. Treat every chance as your best chance and do it to your best. Sincerity in work, integrity in action, commitment to the task and honest approach will always lead to success.

EPITOME OF EXCELLENCE

C. G. Borde

Panther on the Prowl

The hunt was about to begin; the jungle grew silent and tense in apprehension and the intimidating presence of the Panther added to the intrigue. The prey was out there; shrewd and agile, not really up for a grab but only if the hunter is capable. It is actually a battle of wits between the hunter and the hunted and all depended on who outsmarted the other. The Panther silent, strong, athletic, hungry and lithe started to slither slowly yet steadily. The jungle began to watch in hushed anticipation and unabated expectation. The prey was alert and no less smart; conscious and sensitive, it was making its moves to outsmart the Panther. The game has just begun as the panther began to trail the prey and follow its every move with alertness and readiness to strike at the most opportune time.

Finally, the prey lost its nerve and made a dash and seizing the moment, the panther leapt out of its hiding and charged with lightening speed and before the prey could clear the open patch to escape into the jungle, it pounced for the kill. Pandemonium broke loose and the jungle was all agog with noise.

In the midst of the concrete jungle, thousands of spectators were on their feet, as Chandu charged from the long on boundary with unexpected agility to seize the ball flying in the air in what should be a probable six, to send his prey back to the pavilion. Nicknamed "Panther" by his team mates for his fielding excellence, he struck fear in the hearts of his opponents, with his agility, fitness, stamina and speed; he was no less than a "Panther on the Prowl".

Always a contributor, Chandu was well known as a consistent performer with his bat, ball or on the field stopping runs and seizing catches out of nowhere. Indeed, he travelled a long way in a journey that is not only fascinating but filled with twists and turns, adventure and excitement, disappointments and success, acknowledgement and recognition. Coming from a nondescript background, the manner in which he made best of the circumstances to his advantage will indeed be a source of inspiration to many.

Invariably challenging circumstances often challenge a person to seek an answer. While some people find alternatives that give options and explore them, some merely stand aside. This is an attribute that distinguishes those who shine in spite of difficulties as against those who either give up or thrive only under favorable conditions. In Chandu's case, the word "favorable" was not in the dictionary of early life.

Experiencing the True Terror

It is always said that the battle is first fought in the mind and to win a war one has to attack and demoralize the mind of the enemy. West Indies knew it very well and adopted this strategy in the first test match in 1958 at Brabourne stadium. The newspapers were already overboard with write ups about the phenomenal fast bowling of the West Indies team which rattled the day lights out of England on their home turf. Pictures of famed names like Wesley Hall, Taylor, Gilchrist and Conrad in aggressive bowling actions were a common feature and so was a debate. The awesome reputation preceding these names made its impact, making the Indian side squirm in discomfort.

A gigantic Wesley Hall started his run up from the side screen beyond the boundary line, the scene was quite terrifying; a dark 6ft 4in hefty muscular man, with front buttons of his shirt open and a gold chain swaying as he ran with hair flying all over was a picture that could put best of batsmen under pressure. India won the toss and elected to bat and for Chandu Borde, it was his debut.

Unlike today Chandu recalls "there were no helmets, elbow pads, thigh pads, and chest guards. There was no restriction on the number of bouncers or beamers that a bowler could bowl. It was in reality, a life and death situation where one felt as if we were before a firing squad about to be shot".

Fear was indeed the key. It was Pankaj Roy to face Wesley Hall and the first ball he bowled with such speed and length that it went over the heads of the batsman and the wicket keeper landing near the boundary. The impact was terrific and the terror struck; Indian batsmen were unable to cope up. As wickets tumbled, it was Chandu's turn to go out to play. A day he had looked forward to all his life was right here and it seemed that he dreaded it. He recollects "I walked to the crease and tried to get my guard for the middle stump. I was so scared; my hand was violently trembling thus moving the bat from off stump to leg stump. The umpire laughed and said "which one do I give, obviously not all the three; keep the bat from trembling". In any case, he failed miserably in his debut match. The next match, was no different, the West Indies won with ease. He was dropped in the third test but was given a chance again in the fourth one because he was a very good fielder. The test was at Chennai. The first innings, the story repeated with Chandu getting bowled out for a paltry score. He was depressed and aware, that if this trend continued, his future as a test player would end very soon. That day, his elder brother came to see him at the hotel. Seeing his depressed body language, he enquired as to what could be the cause. Chandu told him about the difficulty in facing the fast bowlers and the possibility of his test career coming to an unceremonious end. His brother asked him to sit with him and they prayed together for some time. Somehow this had a calming effect on Chandu. He says "I felt a sense of bravado; I thought I should face them and attack. If I succeed, its fine or else in any case everything was lost. This gave me courage." For the first time, he batted without fear, scoring more than 50 runs. After this, he never looked backand in the next test he scored 109, his first century in the first innings and a 96 in the second. Chandu firmly believes that this turning point occurred because of his grit and the strength he derived from prayers. This sealed the presence of Chandu as he was able to demonstrate a very high sense of resolve, determination and courage in the face of tough challenge. He proved it not by absence of fear but in spite of it.

Rising from Nowhere

Chandu was born in Pune; his father was a policeman. The family was very large with five brothers and four sisters. He grew up in police lines at Somwarpeth. The house was small and the resources were limited. Managing a big family of 11 people with a meager salary of a policeman was a challenge for his parents. Somehow, issues such as this never really bothered Chandu. Happy with the surroundings and with whatever they had, he began his first experiments with cricket. He recalls his own kin were so many that they could play a match with the rest of the children. There were no bats, no wickets and of course no question of any gear. They used a plank as a bat, cork tied with a twine dipped in water to add weight as a cricket ball and the nearest wall with lines drawn as wickets. A scene most common in India where, thousands of kids play cricket in every conceivable way in every conceivable fashion every day. Chandu's family had to move from Somwarpeth on account of his father's transfer to Wadgaon. It was decided to leave Chandu and his elder brother with his uncle who worked at YMCA, in order to enable them to continue with their education.

This was the most important happening in the life of Chandu. It is here, he got to see real cricket. Every day, morning and evening the YMCA team would practice and Chandu would be present there to assist in laying the mat, running for the ball and fielding and erecting the nets etc. Soon he started bowling to members who came in early. He accompanied the YMCA team on Sundays for their matches and always assisted the team during bowling and fielding practices. The Captain of the team was Penton, who was an off spinner and Salve was a leg spinner; these two impressed him enough to make him take up bowling as a leg spinner. He recollects "The possibility of learning batting was a bit difficult since I would never get a chance to bat; I was quite happy to be a bowler".

One Sunday, in an important league match at New English School grounds, one of the players of YMCA team fell sick. Since the team was short of one player, Penton called Chandu to join. Chandu was in his pajamas (loose fitting informal two piece garment usually used for lounging), with slippers and a loose shirt. He did not possess any cricketing gear. Throughout the day, Chandu contributed with full commitment in the field. Penton in appreciation, called Chandu and gave him the ball to bowl. It was an unexpected bonus and thrilled Chandu bowled his heart out and ended up with three wickets. He came home excited and told everybody about this achievement but cricket was not a game they understood, so the response was lukewarm.

Next day something happened that changed the perception of his family towards Chandu and cricket. The Monday Sakal newspaper carried an item which said "Chandu Borde gets Three Wickets". Seeing Chandu's name in the newspaper excited and exhilarated the family for whom this was a wonder beyond words. Chandu became a celebrity in their eyes and they started to encourage him.

The Beginning

Some seemingly innocuous instances always become significant in shaping the direction of life and this news coverage was one of them. Around this time, Chandu started playing for his school. In his very first match, he scored a century and he became a hero in his school. Recognition and appreciation started to add to his reputation steadily and very soon, he started getting calls to substitute in league matches on Sundays by various teams. Thus started the exposure to the cricket league of Pune.

Opportunities just knock once and those who can respond are rewarded with an open door which provides avenues for stepping ahead. One day, he got a call from Nelson, Captain of the National Club, to play for them in a match against the Poona Club. The match was to be played in the Poona Club grounds, these were two very good teams of that time. poona Club was lead by Nagarwala, known for his discipline and sportsmanship. Chandu played and performed well. That day in the evening, Nelson met Nagarwala at the club and over the meal, he asked Nagarwala as to what he thought about Chandu Borde. Nagarwala replied that he was quite impressed and on hearing this, Nelson asked him, "Why don't you take this boy in the Poona Club team? He is from a poor background but very talented. Under you, he can get learning which will benefit him in future". Instantly, Nagarwala asked Nelson to inform Chandu to report to the nets daily.

When Nelson broke this news to Chandu, he found it too incredible to be true. To be part of Poona Club, under the wings of Nagarwala was not even in his wildest of dreams. Ecstatic and overjoyed, Chandu took to this opportunity with all his enthusiasm and commitment. He used to be the first one to be present for the net practice and the last one to leave, never missing a single day.

Practice, persistence, commitment and diligence were the qualities embedded in Chandu that enabled him to learn cricket the way he did. There were no coaches those days and whatever one had to learn by observation and self learning. Chandu never let an opportunity pass by and whatever came his way, he grabbed with both hands.

The First Upgrade

It was time for selection of Maharashtra team for the Ranji Trophy. This was the level which provided a platform for a player to forge ahead. Nagarwala was the chairman of the selection committee and he told the members "I want two players to be included from my side. Rest you people select and I have no objections. The first one is Baba Sidhe and the other is Chandu Borde". The members were surprised at Chandu's name as he was hardly 16 years old. They tried to argue that the first match was against the mighty Bombay team and exposing a young player may result in negative consequences. They said that opportunity can be given at a later date when he would be ready. Nagarwala did not relent and Chandu Borde was included in the team. It was a make or break for Chandu; up against the strongest Ranji team, he was under close watch by many. Fortunately he performed very well with the bat, ball and in the field and the next day's paper read "Wonder Boy of Pune" and for Chandu the flood gates seemed to have opened. He was felicitated publicly at his school and was a hero of sorts in Pune. The Ranji innings had begun well.

His performances were good that year and he came under the lens of one gentleman called Jat Maharaj who was related to the Maharajah of Baroda. Those days, the Maharajah of Baroda's team played for Ranji trophy. Jat Maharaj informed the Maharajah about Chandu Borde. He told him that the boy has immense talent and potential and should be made to play for Baroda. He further told him that Chandu belonged to a poor family and if he stays in Maharashtra, opportunities for his growth were very limited. The Maharajah asked Vijay Hazare, a well respected name in cricket to meet Chandu and offer him a place in the Baroda team and that too with a monthly salary. Chandu joined Baroda and was fortunate to learn from players like Vijay Hazare. His performances with Baroda attracted the attention of the national selectors and within two years, Chandu was called for the annual selection trails camp at Bombay in 1954.

For Chandu, happiness knew no bounds. To him it appeared that Gods were conspiring with destiny in his favor. Enthused and inspired, Chandu gave everything and spared no effort. Six hours of practice, one hour of running in the morning and practicing on his own, he sweated out. The result was obvious, the day of reckoning had come and at barely 18 years of age, he became the youngest player to be part of the team selected for the tour of Pakistan in 1954.

Still under twenty, Chandu, son of a policeman, with humble economic status and meager resources to support; no background to the game in which he wanted to excel; no one to coach, with just a dream in his eyes and hard work as his gift, blessed with a talent that just evolved with effort; here he was at the threshold of a great career. The horizon was visible but he looked to be looking beyond.

Career and Beyond

Though the Pakistan tour was his maiden tour, he did not get a chance to make his debut. This would happen much later with the West Indies in 1958. The series of West Indies started with a disaster for Chandu but ended with a resounding success due to his ability to bounce back with resurgence. With this began, an unending affair with cricket.

Starting as young as twenty, he got an opportunity to play in England in their County Cricket. He became a frequent visitor to England. His schooling was left behind as he started to pursue cricket with passion and thus he found himself in a tight situation in the initial days when it became difficult for him to understand and speak in English. Chandu was not the one to give up, he observed, attempted, practiced and finally succeeded. He mastered the English language and very soon could be a part of every conversation. In spite of his drawbacks on account of his background and education, he was respected and treated with regard because of his discipline, dedication and commitment to the team he represented. Chandu says "I must have been to England more than 20 times. Playing in the county matches made me a much better player as I could learn the art of facing fast bowling in conditions ideal for pace and also fine tune my bowling and fielding. "

Anecdotes and Incidents are always an integral part of any illustrious career. Chandu always better known as a batsman and a fielder, had a latent talent in bowling too. It was in the first test match against England, that he came out with his best teaming with Salim Durrani. Durrani, an off spinner and Chandu as a leg spinner combined effectively to take 14 wickets between them resulting in India winning the match. Their contribution was such , that it made England team very vulnerable to spin and India won the series. Both Durrani and Chandu were aptly nicknamed as "Spin Twins"

His outstanding performance with the bat against Pakistan at Madras in 1962, was his highest score in test cricket at 177 not out was also an exhibition of elegance and display of cricket at its best.

Chandu had a fruitful career and unlike many who walk away into oblivion, he chose to be associated with the game. Knowing his standing and reputation for integrity, he was appointed Manager of the Indian Cricket team which toured Pakistan in 1989. Amongst the team members was a very young boy and his name was Sachin Tendulkar, who was just 16 years of age. Chandu remembers an incident which mirrored the future of Sachin. The match was at Sialkot and Pakistan's Waquar Younus was bowling at his best. One sharp delivery rose up and hit Sachin on the lip. The play was stopped as there was bleeding and Chandu rushed to the field to look at the young boy. After the treatment on field, Chandu suggested to Sachin to quit the game and come back. Sachin refused and assured Chandu that he can manage and the next three balls of Waquar, he drove to the boundary. This fearless and determined attitude, Chandu felt was the key to Sachin's success.

Another Incident relating to Sachin, when Chandu was the manager is relevant from the perspective of understanding the meaning of focus, learning attitude and thirst for runs. This happened in 2007, by this time Sachin was already a legend. The test was at Scotland and Sachin was out for a paltry score of less than 10 runs twice. As he came back to the dressing room thinking why it happened, Chandu told him "the ball you played, should have been played to "Mid-on" not "Mid-wicket". Next day, at the net practice, Sachin requested Chandu to bowl and he practiced the shot towards Midon. Chandu was deeply impressed by his willingness to learn even at the point when he was considered the best in the world. These qualities, he feels are the one's needed to succeed in life.

As a manager, Chandu was highly respected and regarded He says "I owe this to my upbringing as a cricketer with the Baroda team under Vijay Hazare. Vijay Hazare was a "Gentlemen's Gentleman". His very presence had an electrifying effect and his conduct was simply exquisite. He would always talk to every player with gentle courteousness yet firm and strong without raising his voice or offending anyone. It was not as if he was soft, he had that ability to drive home his point without humiliating anyone". Chandu feels this learning experience shaped his conduct, behavior and attitude which not only helped him as a player but also as a Manager and later as Chairman of the selection committee.

Having had an innings which gave him many a respectable positions, one position seems to have eluded Chandu. He represented India for 12 years from 1958 to 1970. He played 55 test matches with 5 centuries including 177 not out scored against Pakistan.

A dream to lead the Indian team as a Captain was indeed the most befitting acknowledgment any player would aspire for and Chandu was no exception. Fully experienced as an all rounder, a disciplined cricketer, consistent contributor and performer, it was no surprise when he was called and informally told by the selection committee chairman that he was selected as the Captain of the Indian team. The news called for a celebration and Chandu borrowed money and took his fellow cricketers for dinner. Next day as he was ready to face the press for the announcement, the Captain was changed and a different name was announced; Chandu stood aghast in disbelief and disappointment. Political influence was rampant those days and he became a victim of politics being denied the deserving role of captaincy, as instructions from top political leadership took away the one time opportunity for Chandu.

This influenced him to such an extent that he resolved never to succumb to pressure and ensure integrity in every decision. This approach endeared him to all as a manager and later as a selector. He resisted pressures by refusing to compromise selections made on merit. As a firm believer in talent, performance and ability to contribute as key factors for selection, he never wavered from this.

The match against England was very significant. The selection committee was in the process of finalizing the team. Chandu was keen on selecting a young upcoming cricketer named Azharuddin for his debut at Calcutta. Sunil Gavaskar was the captain, who expressed his reservations, since playing before a very huge charged up crowd like Calcutta would be a daunting experience for a new comer. Sunil suggested that Azhar be given an opportunity later. Chandu felt that Azhar had a strong combination of batting and fielding which enhanced his potential and "went ahead with his choice, which proved to be right as Azhar scored three successive centuries in the first three tests he played. This incident similar to the one he faced early in his career, which probably influenced the thinking of Chandu. He always believed that team players are more important than individual centric ones. An all-rounder was his most preferred choice, not because he was one but because "An all-rounder can always contribute; with his bat, ball and in the field. "The selection of the 1983 world cup team which won the trophy is an apt example of selection of good all-rounders". That team had six all-rounders and the outcome is of course part of cricketing history.

Reflections and Thoughts

The fact that Chandu served the Cricket Board in various capacities for 25 years is a testimony of faith, integrity, commitment and acceptability by the cricketing fraternity. Chandu feels "Always remaining honest, having the interest of the country and ensuring opportunity to the most deserving are the significant factors" which gave him such undisputed respect and regard. He has very high aspirations and hopes from the current generation of cricketers. He feels they are very disciplined, focused and hard working. The competition has made it more competitive and there is a definite shift in the approach towards the game. But beneath all the changes in techniques and approach, the basics remains the same. While one has to learn the game of cricket by the book to develop the art, one must also play by instinct which is a reflection of talent.

The current game though highly commercialized, has a bright future as each format contributes to the overall growth of the game. Twenty-Twenty improves fielding and running between the wickets along with creation of scope for innovation. One day internationals focus on variation in bowling and the test matches enable variation in strokes and retaining the art form of cricket. A cricketer playing all the three formats has to go through tremendous of amount of mental preparation as every game has its share of hurdles for the batsman.

As a player, selector, manager, he was known for his value based behavior. He attributes his strong sense of values and empathy to his background and to his mother. He vividly recollects how she used to keep a part of her food for Chandu since he would come back tired after long hours of practice. Growing up in such circumstances always adds to the maturity, creates more understanding and concern for others than self. A manifestation of this was clearly perceptible in Chandu throughout his career.

Chandu always held Vijay Hazare as a model of excellence in conduct and behavior. He recognizes Fathesingh Rao Gaikwad, Maharajah of Baroda as yet another example of being a gentleman. He feels one must always look for role models and emulate them. A firm believer that success is never an effort of an individual. It's a combination of support and opportunity given by many. Having gratitude to those who created opportunity is very important to remain grounded and humble.

At this old age, he looks as energetic and enthused as a man of thirties. The charm of goodness exudes from his presence and one can tell that "Cricket" still remains very much his life line. The very mention of this word lights up his face and one can be part of that infective enthusiasm. Having been an example of exemplary professional conduct, Chandu will always rule the hearts of art lovers of cricket as one who has and who will forever symbolize an "Epitome of Excellence"

■ ■ ■

Key Learning Values

Opportunities are Always Hidden: Most opportunities do not come with name tag. They are always hidden beyond what one can see. One must seek, identify and exploit or else someone else will do so.

A Chance Lost is Never The Last Chance: It is always the law of nature to lose many chances that come our way. It is important to understand that one lost chance is never the last chance.

Persistence and Dedication: These attributes are fundamental to success. One must begin, continue, pursue and persist. In the absence of these attributes, opportunities will become missed opportunities.

Do the Best: Do not wait for that right moment to do the best. Whatever you begin to do, do it with the best effort and rest will surely follow.

Understanding Importance of Values In Life: A person is a success only when he is valued as a person. This cannot happen unless one understands the importance of values and behavior.

Facing The Adversity: In life, every individual has to go through adversities. How well one tackles these to rise above them will determine how successful one gets to be. Have courage to face them up front.

Humble Yet Strong: In success, retain humility and in difficulty display strength of character. This combination in any individual will bring out the very best always.

P. P. Chhabria

Education is independent of qualification. Be open minded to learn, be positive to accept and believe that everything and anything is possible and never believe the impossible.

TREADING BEYOND CIRCUMSTANCES

P. P. Chhabria

Feisty in Spirit

Travelling across India, alone in a third class compartment for a teenage boy could well be a challenge. In late 1940's, the rail and road communications in India were quite rudimentary. Connectivity was limited and comforts were not many. Travel was in a way, a necessity rather than pleasure. Beginning his career as a domestic helper at the age of 12 in Karachi, Prahalad was around 14 years of age, as he boarded the train at Amritsar on that fateful day. He was going home to Karachi after spending a year or so, working for traders who sold wholesale goods. Prahalad was earning a "Princely" sum of Rs 20 per month for the job of collecting and accounting the money from customers. As he left his employers shop, he was given a ten rupee note. The note those days was large in size and possibly was worth the value of a thousand today. He was indeed thrilled to possess one and he examined the same with a lot of care and pride. The number on the note attracted him, he inadvertently memorized the same. Sometimes, some things happen which lead to unexpected outcomes in the most unusual situations.

It is human psychology, to reach out to things that are precious to us. A pat on the pocket, frequent glances to confirm and checking the place where things are kept, certain degree of discomfort on the face and many more symptoms manifest the behavior, when a person is conscious. These actions invariably indicate a sense of nervousness that usually accompanies when something precious is carried on person. To an expert eye, it is quite easy to detect and thus such people fall prey to petty thieves who were in abundance those days. For Prahalad, the ten rupee note on him was no less than a treasure and it had to be shielded from the eyes of thieves, he thought. He rolled it around and put it in the left pocket of his pajamas and fell asleep as the train moved along. The train had to pass through Larkhana Station in Pakistan. He woke up with a jolt as the train came to a halt and instinctively he reached for the pocket only to be aghast to find his treasure missing. Prahalad raised a hue and cry and a compassionate conductor tried to assuage him. Prahalad insisted that the Pathan in front of him be searched. The conductor asked him "even if I find a ten rupee note, how can you prove that the note is yours"? Prahalad told him the number of the note he had memorized. Hearing that, the Pathan owned up having stolen the money. Prahalad got down at the station, filed a complaint and hired a lawyer to represent him in the court. Those days, such cases were dealt on a daily basis by a Magistrate. The Pathan pleaded guilty and was awarded few months of imprisonment. Prahalad had to negotiate the lawyer's fee too which he managed to keep it at two rupees and in the end returned victorious with eight rupees in his pocket. What is simply amazing is the way a boy hardly fourteen dealt with such a situation. Maturity beyond age, fearless and bold, he displayed bravado with a sense of relentless pursuit to ensure the culprit was punished. This indeed was an indication of the future in store.

Riches to Rags

Good fortune always blinds the cruelty of fate and fatality of future. When times are good rarely can one think of how bad it can be if the tide gets turned. That's the nature of human behavior and thinking. Though not always, fate does play a cruel joke on some. It strikes with such intensity, to shatter the placid complacent sense of well being. Such harsh realities become turning points for resurrection for some and symbolize the final desolation for others.

Prahalad was a blessed child or so it seemed. Born in a very rich family, he grew up in the lap of luxury. His father owned a big bungalow with a retinue of servants to attend to every need. Though the family was big with five brothers and five sisters, the bungalow was large enough to accommodate all with every comfort one could seek. Prahalad was always attended upon by many servants. He was quite a pampered child who needed servants to assist him to take a bath. In the midst of such a comfortable life, Prahalad never really thought that he should focus on studies and neither did any one compel him to do so. In those days, children went to school around 7 years of age. Prahalad showed no interest or inclination to study and his formal education was almost at a naught after he completed his II standard. The affluence was such; that it just did not matter.

Things changed when his father suddenly passed away due to heart attack in 1942. His elder brothers took over the business and found themselves grossly ill equipped to manage. The task seemed onerous and the work very hard. They were influenced by fair weather friends who misguided them with their suggestions to invest money in speculation as a means for earning easy and fast. Intoxicated by the desire for a fast buck, his brothers steadily lost all the wealth, land, property and even the bungalow. In no time the family was literally on streets, having lost everything. From the opulence of plenty to the paucity of poverty; the transformation from "Riches to Rags" was complete.

For young Prahalad, the change was too fast and too difficult. To understand the situation and bear with the discomforts was tough and emotionally traumatic. In spite of this unwanted change, Prahalad found himself to be better equipped to face the trauma. Since, he did not show any interest in studies, his brother made him work in a cloth shop for a wage of Rs10 per month. He was expected to work throughout the day from 10 am to 8 pm and for seven days a week as there was no concept of a holiday like we have now on Sundays. He was required to clean the shop, serve the customers with lassi (Cold Sweet buttermilk) or sharbat (Cold drink) and look after them. What a change indeed from a child who was pampered and served by servants; to be in the position of a shop boy serving customers. Though hardly 12 years of age, he somehow understood the stark reality as it stared at him; never complained and accepted the present situation with realism. He keenly observed how the customers were treated and how important it was to do so and this became a very important lesson for him.

Prahalad by nature was an observer. He could see much more than others and could analyze much better. This attribute was instrumental in enabling a learning curve in every activity he was involved throughout his life.

He worked with the cloth merchant for year or so. Thereafter, he shifted to another job which paid him Rs15 per month. The next jump came, when he got a job with a contractor, to sit next to his driver to protect pilferage of petrol. This continued for a year before his brother found a job for him with the whole sale dealers in Amritsar and thus he moved on. He was put through series of jobs as time passed by. In 1945, came the first opportunity to seek better pastures. Prahalad moved to Pune to work for a money lender.

Building Brick by Brick

Pune in 1945 was green, salubrious, devoid of sweltering heat and chilling cold that prevails across North India. Small roads, carts and vendors, shops and stalls dotted across the localities added a resplendent charm to the town which seemed captivating. During those days, Pune was politically very active from the independence movement point of view, with many leaders of repute emerging from this city. The city exuded a feel of vibrancy, a touch of class, a tinge of cosmopolitan culture; blend of polite behavior coupled with refined and enlightened environs created an inimitable experience for young Prahalad.

The population was no more than a lakh and there were hardly any motor vehicles. Being close to the port city of Bombay, the town was the emerging nerve center of business, culture and education. It is in this city, Prahalad, stepped in to be greeted by a different culture, language and social environment to which he adapted ardently.

For about two years he worked with the money lender and managed to save Rs 1000. By this time, the situation in Lahore was getting tense, with the possibility of partition looming large. It was the beginning of 1947 and Prahalad's elder brother decided to move the entire family to Pune. He asked Prahalad to take a house on rent and on conformation, the entire family consisting of four brothers, three sisters; his mother and grandmother arrived in Pune. The house he hired was, 485, Narayan Peth, consisted of three rooms for a monthly rent of Rs 30.

His elder brother moved to Bombay to take up a job and the rest stayed back in Pune. The money he saved was not adequate to support a large family and there was a need to look for better earning opportunities. At this juncture, he was introduced to an electrical goods manufacturer who was looking for a dealer to sell his products in Pune. Prahalad seized this opportunity and secured a dealership. He stared selling these products and very soon understood the need for setting up a shop and went on to establish it opposite Jogeshwari Temple. One and a half years later, understanding the need to expand, he moved over to a bigger space at 675 Budhwar Peth. The business was good but the earnings were just about adequate. Prahalad realized that if he has to grow, he needs to look for more options. During these years, as part of his sales beat, he met many customers who had a requirement of bulk purchase; he also observed that many organizations required continuous supply on a contractual basis. To Prahalad, this seemed a good prospect to explore and he applied for registration as a supply contractor. On approval of his registration, he went about very diligently seeking out tenders and made attempts to secure contracts. The initial contracts came from the defence services; 512 Army Base Workshop at Kirkee, Pune awarded a contract which subsequently paved the way for large supply contracts to army establishments up to Delhi. He supplied a wide variety of electrical goods including a large amount of cable. In a span of just four years, he accumulated a saving of over 3 lakhs, which was very substantial in those days. Hardly 25 years of age, it began to look as though he was on his way up; from a moneylender's shop in 1945 to a prosperous supplier of electrical goods by 1955 was a huge change. He realized the importance of some attributes which are a must to grow in business. "Hard work and relentless pursuit, timely delivery, adherence to quality of supplies and aspiration for honest profit". With this realization, he began to look ahead.

By this time, Prahalad could sense the increasing business avenues. He realized that the scope in the supply of cable and was on a look out to find a way to get a better way to deal with it. This came about in 1956, at the International Industrial Exhibition at Delhi. There, he saw a cable manufacturing machine for Rs 50000 and immediately purchased it. He also got a license on the spot as the government was promoting manufacturing of some specific products and cable was one of them. Prahalad also managed to get DGS & D approval which gave him access to defence and public sector undertakings. On his return to Pune, he had to find a space to establish a factory and install the machinery. At Karve road, he found a shed which belonged to the brother of Nathuram Godse, and approached him to rent it out for him. Here the first factory of Prahalad was established, with technical expertise from his younger brother Mr. K. P. Chhabria. With the establishment of this factory, he shifted his entire operations to Karve road premises next to the river which became a boon of sorts.

Since the cable became his product, he realized that creating a distinct product image in the form of brand was necessary. Thus came the name "Finolex" representing "Fine" for quality "Flex" for flexibility and "O" symbolizing a connect This was early 1960's when terms like brand and branding were still unknown in India. Prahalad in any case had no exposure to management jargon or education. All he knew was that, he needed to create something special in the minds of his customers which represented quality, durability and trust. He knew that such a name should be independent of the company and must be distinctive. Shrewd observation and keen understanding of business was instrumental in Prahalad's fine acumen.

The Turning Tide

The tide began to turn. As manufacturing became a reality, Prahalad embarked on a focused mission to market his products. He would travel extensively and initially targeted South India and Bombay. As demands grew, he found that Karve road establishment was inadequate and the need for setting up a full scale plant had to be addressed. Just before the catastrophic Panshet Dam burst in Pune the entire plant was shifted to Pimpri where He had purchased 10 acres of land along with another 15 acres adjacent to it. In the 25 acre plot stands Finolex as a testimony of effort, excellence and commitment of Prahalad. What started as a dealership, went on to a small scale enterprise and then grew up to be a manufacturing giant in cables, wires and pipes in a short span of time. From one manufacturing unit today, there are nine across India and Finolex as a brand stands for immense credibility.

In 1962, Prahalad did something which very few especially in business do. Late Morarji Desai and Yashwant Rao Chavan, both most respected political leaders of that time met Prahalad and requested him to sell the 10 acre plot next to his factory to Garware's, a well respected industrial family of Pune, who were in need of it. Prahalad gave away the prime

10 acres at the very same price he purchased and not at market price not out of magnanimity but as a matter of principle.

As the company began to expand, need for more space arose. Prahalad came to know of a company called Alpha Rubber at Lonavala was up for sale. He utilized this chance and acquired this company and merged it with Finolex. Since this was a registered company in stock exchange, it made it easy for Finolex to seek permission to go public and Finolex went public in 1972 which was oversubscribed 16 times. Those were the days when the public participation in business was very restricted and public viewed investments in primary/secondary markets with skepticism. The fact that he could attract such investment is a reflection of the credible brand name he could build along with consistent profitability and dividends. He also became the first entrepreneur to have entered into a Joint venture with Israel. Finolex is the first Indian company to have such a joint-venture and have set up Finolex Plasson Industries Ltd. FPIL offers wide range of products and solutions in the field of precise Irrigation and Intensive Agriculture Cultivation. The solutions include complete tailored Drip and Micro Sprinkler Systems and Turn-Key projects for agriculture sectors.

In acknowledgement to his services in extending and promoting business relations with Israel, he received an "Award of Honour" from the Prime Minister of Israel, Mr. Ehud Olmert at a glittering ceremony held in Jerusalem, Israel, on 12 November 2008.

Prahalad also moved to resin, which was mostly imported. He made a foray into this field and sought permission to establish a plant. To set up this plant, he needed a captive port and hence acquired 800 acres of land at Ratnagiri. Today, Finolex is Number one in India in pipes and cables and only a close second behind Reliance Industries in resin. Born in the year 1930 and from being a domestic helper at the age of twelve, barely literate, Prahalad P Chhabria built Finolex to what it is today - a well diversified professionally managed conglomerate with interests in total cables solutions, Petrochemicals, PVC Resin, Pipes & Fittings, Agricultural Drip Irrigation systems, and Education. Today more than 5,000 families are part of the Finolex family by way of employment across its twelve manufacturing facilities in Uttarakhand, Maharashtra and Goa. To cater to the international markets, Finolex has set up an office in Dubai.

Managing and Living

In spite of all these achievements and the success in business, the personal front had its share of ups and downs. For a man who worked as if possessed, managing time for family wife, son Prakash and two daughters Aruna and Sonali would always be a challenge. His wife Mohini played a crucial role in ensuring that he was left free to pursue his mission of building Finolex. Swami RamBaba met Prahalad more by accident than design. He was 114 years old at that time. He used to stay at Prahalad's house whenever he would come to Pune and was a great source of mentoring and had a calming effect on him. The very first day Swami Ram Baba met his younger daughter Sonali, he told him that something was seriously wrong with her. On medical examination, it was revealed that she suffered from blood cancer. Prahalad did everything a father could to get her treated. Swami Ram Baba accompanied his wife and daughter to USA for his daughter's treatment. His wife stayed on for nine months in a hotel with his daughter. But alas! Sonali did not survive and passed away. Unable to recover from this shock, his wife too passed away. This emotional trauma was tough for Prahalad but he realized that life must go on and he must make the best of it by doing the best for people.

The focus began to shift from "doing well to doing good." He realized that if the country is to evolve, two aspects need to be addressed, firstly, education for all and secondly, healthcare for all. He passionately took up these two areas and began building schools and colleges to offer quality education at subsidized fees. He began to advocate free education for all till college level and free medical care for all to be a mandatory part of CSR policy. At Ratnagiri, he built a world class engineering college Finolex Academy of Management & Technology (FAMT) at present there are 2400 students studying in 6 B.E. Programs and 2 Postgraduate Programs. The Mukul Madhav Vidyalaya, Ratnagiri launched in the memory of his grandson Mukul Madhav, was the first English medium primary school established in Ratnagiri. This Vidyalaya proved to be a boon to the societal need of the at Ranpar-Golap and most of its students are from the lower income strata of the society. Spread across 10 acres of land the ambitious school project was launched in 2010 and is being run on a charity basis for classes from pre-primary to twelveth standard, thus catering to the educational needs of the underdeveloped coastal area in Maharashtra. He also set up the International Institute of Informtion and Technology (I^2IT) in Pune. I^2IT was dedicated to the nation at the hands of Shri A. P. J. Abdul Kalam, Honorable Former President of India on May 28, 2003. At I^2IT, He introduced 14 programs in association with well known foreign universities and enrolled professors of Indian origin from USA to come and teach students to give them exposure to world class education at less than one fourth the cost. He regrets that All India Council for Technical Education placed a bar on this project and compelled him to close. It's a battle he is still fighting as he feels, it helps hundreds of students who do not have the financial capacity to go abroad and study. At present, I^2IT offers undergraduate engineering degree courses of 4 years duration in the areas of Electronics & Telecommunication, Computer Science and Information Technology affiliated to the University of Pune and is recognized by All India Council for Technical Education (AICTE), New Delhi and Govt. of Maharashtra. Over the years, there have been more than 3,000 I^2IT alumni have gone on to pursue their careers in various industries or academics (by enrolling for Ph.D.s).

For his outstanding leadership, Finolex was presented the Harvard Business School and Economic Times Award for the Best Corporate

Performance and also has been recognised as one of the Hidden Champions of the World by World Link Magazine published by World Economic Forum, Geneva. He was honored by Chairman of UK-India Business Council Lord Karan Bilimoria on 6 May 08 at the prestigious Institute of Directors in London with a silver platter in recognition of his contribution to 'Entrepreneurship'. Hard Work, dedication, quality service and integrity have been key factors that have given Prahalad an eminent place among the nation's industrialists. He is the recipient of many prominent awards in India and abroad.

To him, serving the community assumes much more significance and feels that as much resources as possible must be utilized for the larger good. These are not just words which are hollow but are reinforced by something he has done which very few would do.

Prahalad has willed his entire group of companies to be converted to a Trust after his death with a hope that the Finolex Group of Companies will continue forever. A decision he says has made many unhappy but he stands by it as he feels that best can be done only by sacrifice. Prahalad has indeed walked much more than the talk.

How did he do what he did? What would he tell the younger generation as a takeaway from his own life "I will tell them never ever look down on what you can do; Never feel that you had nothing to inherit so nothing can be done; Never feel that education is only through qualification; Be open minded, Be positive to believe that everything and anything is possible and never believe the impossible."

From ten rupees to six thousand crores, from a boy who cleaned the shops to be the founder of a diversified group, from a young man fighting for survival to a man of vision and magnanimity, from a three room house to two acre bungalow, from an astute business man to generous philanthropist. Prahalad has journeyed through the thick and thin braving the fire and rain. Every time a circumstance beckoned him, he moved ahead never to hesitate, never to shy and always "Treading Beyond Circumstances" seeking and achieving the seemingly impossible.

■ ■ ■

Key Learning Values

Look Beyond Problems: To meet the challenges of life, one must not be weighed down by problems but make an effort to look beyond as there is always light at the end of the tunnel.

Observe the Unobserved: It is said that one does not need new landscapes but needs new eyes. Observation is the best teacher.

Be Without Self Pity: Looking at what is not with us results in self pity. Look at what you have and it will tell how to use it. Never crib or compare.

Make Your Own Course: Success is making out your own course. Moving along a beaten track may lead to the end but not your destination.

Integrity and Quality: A very important attribute in every action one takes. Reputations are built by these two qualities.

Believe that Anything Can Be Done: A do or die attitude with strong purpose is the solution to any problem.

Lila Poonawalla

In life one must adopt a "mirror, window and a door approach". Mirror tp show what one is capable of; window to show what the world has to offer; door to show the skill sets to acquire to walk out to meet the challenges.

ALWAYS A STEP AHEAD

Lila Poonawalla

Tryst with Destiny

"It was the best of times, it was the worst of times, it was the age of wisdom, it was the age of foolishness, it was the epoch of belief, it was the epoch of incredulity, it was the season of Light, it was the season of darkness, it was the spring of hope, it was the winter of despair, we had everything before us, we had nothing before us….." The aftermath of French revolution described by Charles Dickens fits in aptly to the saga of grief which epitomized the dawn of Independence in August of 1947.

As Pandit Jawaharlal Nehru stood before the first constituent assembly, his eloquent words were to symbolize a new era of optimism "At the stroke of the midnight hour as the whole world sleeps, India awakens to freedom, a moment comes but rarely in history when the soul of a nation long suppressed finds its utterance". As independence dawned on India and Pakistan, the sun set on the sanity of people who stood divided in disarray forever by the partition. A human tragedy of unimaginable consequence was to unfold. Beyond all objectivity, a tide of inconceivable hatred engulfed the people on both sides. Rationalism went to winds, friendship and neighbourhood relations were a figment of imagination, hate blinded their eyes and Hindus, Muslims and Sikhs alike; brothers and friends a few days prior became blood thirsty, like hounds seeking out each other, killing, burning and looting. To those who died in hundreds, to the thousands who lost their homes and millions whose lives lost all semblance of harmony; these were times of distress ushered by a tsunami of hatred. Rendered homeless, devoid of resources, with bare minimum things in tow, a huge sea of humanity crossed across the borders in search of safety, security and a better tomorrow.

Lila was just about three years of age when her family was uprooted from Pakistan. Age was on her side as she was blissfully unaware of the ferocity and grievousness of this traumatic situation. Her grandparents insisted on moving the entire family. Thus Lila accompanied by her mother and five brothers along with some relatives, reached the "Refugee Camp" established at Lonavala.

Bolt from the Blue

ALFA LAVAL (India), then called Vulcan Laval Ltd. was going through tough times. The business was at an all time low and a change in the top leadership was on the cards. The Board began their meeting in Bombay to identify a suitable candidate for the position of CEO and Managing Director. Lila was one of the "Senior General Managers" at that time and was not in the least, one of the contenders in question as there were three Senior Vice Presidents above her to be reckoned with.

A telephone call summoned her to Bombay. As she entered the plush conference room in an up market five star hotel, an unusual premonition ailed her. The Chairman of the Board after discussing the future course to set the company on track, told her that the Board's decision to appoint her as the CEO & MD. An unthinkable had happened. A lady being made CEO & MD for the first time, after overlooking three Senior Vice Presidents, setting an unprecedented precedent in India. Her first instinctive reaction was to refuse because she felt inadequate for this responsibility. Seeking time to think, she came out of the conference room and called her mentor, supporter, guide and husband Firoz and told him her decision to decline the offer. It was Firoz, who rushed to Bombay to convince her to take on this challenge reminding her that her strength lay in seeking challenges and succeeding therefore this challenge should never be let off. Lila thus became the first woman in India to become a CEO & MD of a multinational engineering company and rest that followed was history. Looking back, it has been a long journey; from a refugee camp in Lonavala to the Chamber of MD & CEO was *unbelievable yet true.*

Oblivion is Happiness

For a little girl like Lila, it hardly mattered. Her world revolved around her mother and brothers. The holocaust of partition and the experiences of horror fortunately did not singe her. She stayed in the frugal conditions of the refugee camp, sharing a small space with her entire family. She did not feel the pangs of discomfort which the elders did, having come from an affluent background. The life at the camp was tough; they had to subsist on a meager monthly government subsidy of Rs 40 per month for the entire family and an insurance payout of Rs 40 from her father's policy after his death. He died in a railway accident before Lila arrived in Lonavala.

Those days, she recalls "I was quite carefree and happy wearing the same dress for more than a day, eating a very frugal meal, getting one cup of milk in a week, one egg in ten days and playing with other children at the camp, sharing a small space with family with little or no privacy. Happy because I believed that this is the way of life as everybody else around us lived that way. I think those early years gave me resilience to adapt and adjust which possibly shaped a lot of my thinking and actions as I grew up. I owe it to my mother who had an abundance of positivity which she displayed notwithstanding the trying circumstances and stress" Soon they moved to Pune and the painful process of rebuilding a new life in a new environment under a completely new setting began. Lila was the only girl amongst the children and thus she grew up with her brothers more as a tomboy seeking to be one of them and taking on everything boys did from playing "Gulli Danda" to "Galli Cricket". She was never the one to back out and always took up every challenge boys would fling at her with determination. "Whenever I was told that I was a girl and I should not do or could not do a thing, I would take it on with renewed passion to show that I can and I could". Growing up with boys gave her the confidence to be one among them more as an equal.

Her mother was the pivot around which the family would rally. Always at work, she would do variety of chores from papads & pickle making, stitching etc to augment her meager income. "We fortunately received some financial support from our relatives and family friends, who had businesses in Pune and abroad. They would at times send money and many a times hand down their daughter's (who was of my age) clothes to me. It was very exciting when ever their car would come because it meant some good clothes and dolls for me and may be spending a couple of days in their house to play with their daughter and get goodies to eat and bring home" . It is invariably an influence that makes a significant impact bringing a change. One such influence on Lila was Ms. Sunderjee, her teacher at Mount Caramel. She was in IX standard when Ms. Sunderjee accosted Lila and took her to the staff room.

"Lila, I think you must look at your potential. Not many are blessed with your intelligence and sharpness you possess, do not waste your time, let your potential show and focus on studies. You will be the best." Her words made a profound imprint on Lila and she turned around;

from an average performer to an excellent one, doing well in SSC and HSC and moving onto engineering Her choice to be an engineer met with skepticism and resistance. Every one advised her that it's not a profession for girls and therefore an inappropriate choice. As far as Lila was concerned, greater the resistance greater was the resolve. To top it, she chose mechanical engineering which was considered a male bastion. Just two girls in the class, she was the centre of all attraction and enjoyed her stint in engineering. She recollects "College was an exceptional time. We did not miss out on anything, however small. It was participation, learning, enjoyment and celebration all the way. I would always advise the young to enjoy these days as they are unique and irreplaceable in life".

Journey Through The Glass Ceiling

It was never easy to be among men trying to do what they are used to doing and more importantly trying to demonstrate one is better. Her childhood experience of being among boys was one thing but to crack the myth of women in male dominated technical field was another. Her first taste of bias came to her when her job applications met with deadlock even in companies like Bajaj, TATA's, Firodia, Bharat Forge etc. She finally got an opening in a British company called Ruston and Hornsby. It was here she met Firoz with whom she fell in love. As the company rules prohibited wife and husband working in the same company, she had to quit, since Firoz was in a better position than her in the company. It was through the assistance of her school Physical Training Instructor, Mr. Ellis that she got the job of an apprentice engineer in Alfa Laval, then called Vulcan Laval, a Swedish multinational Company in Pune. She was very keen to work and learn on the shop floor but was prevented from doing so by Mr. Sonalkar, the then Production manager of machine shop. He was Head of the shop floor and refused to admit any women, as he felt it would distract the attention of his workers. She joined the fabrication unit under supervision of Mr. Soli Bharucha, and worked there for almost a year. Later on she got to work in the machine shop only after Mr. Sonalkar left. It was an interesting twist of fate that Mr. Sonalkar's daughter in later years did Mechanical Engineering and he came back to ask Lila to guide and mentor her. Lila recollects "I really liked the way he conceded that it was unfair on his part to have prevented me from working on the shop floor. He did so not because he needed a favor from me for his daughter, but having genuinely realized his approach was inappropriate. I think this was his greatness and I appreciated this very much". Lila recollects another incident quite similar. "The day it was officially declared that I was to take over as CEO & MD of the company, three of my seniors managers, expressed their inability to work under a woman boss and decided to quit. Years later, after the company was turned around, each one of them spoke to her warmly and complimented her while admitting that quitting was probably a decision made in haste". Lila as a leader was always capable of getting the best out of people. *"It's not about getting people who are good to work for you but it's all about making people working with you feel good thus making them give out their best, that is most important. People always respond but how they respond depends on how you treat them".* As a leader, a woman and an eager contributor, she always saw her role as facilitator as she personally evolved in life due to substantial facilitation, support, confidence, trust and undying faith reposed in her by those who mattered. How does one gain and grow in confidence? She narrates "After I was appointed the CEO & MD, as per norm, it was required that I address all the employees at a function. It was organized at the Turf club. I made copious notes and prepared my address. Nervous as I was, I began to read from my notes. The COO of Parent Swedish company, and a director on the board of the Indian subsidiary, Mr. Lars Hallden, who also became my mentor, stopped me and told me that the whole company wanted to hear what I had to say and not what I could read. "So speak from your heart, reach out to them and make them feel what you feel and get your message across. With these words, he took away those sheets of paper, thus leaving me to speak and that made me the person I am today. I realized that to be able to speak from one's heart is more important than speaking from a good script."

Was being a woman a disadvantage? Lila never believed so. She says, it all depends on how one projects oneself. Maintaining dignity, ensuring due decorum in behavior and actions, becoming an example by being exemplary will always lead to greater respect and acceptance. Whether she worked on the shop floor shoulder to shoulder with men or whether she was dealing with companies, customers, superiors and outside environment, her being a woman proved more of an asset and never a disadvantage. The other issue of significance is that women should never undermine themselves because they are women. She always believed this unequivocally and attributes her childhood experiences for such confidence.

One important attribute a leader must demonstrate is forthright commitment to the best interests of the company not towards any individual. She narrates an incident in her work life as an export manager. She had procured a large order from USSR, which required her to import key equipments from overseas. As per the rules of the group all products available within the group companies had to be purchased within the group. The prices of these equipment were almost 30 % higher and also the payment terms not conducive as compared to similar equipment being supplied by companies outside the group. She took this up in a Board meeting, at the risk of even losing her job, where overseas parent company directors were present, she argued that she should be permitted to buy the equipment from outside the group to retain good profit margin for her project. This certainly came as a big surprise to the Foreign Directors and they were reasonably upset with her. She was instructed not to deviate from the norms set by the group, and order the equipment from the companies within in the group. However she was assured that this would be looked into. Soon after she received a communication from Sweden that the parent company has acceded to her request for a reduction in price by 30% and six month credit support. Sometimes as leaders one has to take the "Bull by the Horns" but then the reason has to be sound and facts must be right, and more importantly one has to be ready to face the consequences of the decision.

New Horizons on an Unchartered Path

An illustrious corporate career came to a culmination but the illustrious instinct had not ceased to evolve. Using a substantial portion of her own funds, Lila set about to do something close to her heart. An inner yearning to work for the betterment of women and make a contribution in the field of education and empowerment in enabling a better life. What drove her to this decision? She explained "Probably two significant experiences; firstly, my years at refugee camp followed by our struggle for reviving our lives and secondly, the silent influence of my mother, who withstood and weathered all our storms alone with such fortitude that I realized how much difference women can make in enabling and ensuring a good life for others while giving the best of theirs".

She also attributes her own experiences throughout her career and realized that she could withstand a lot because she had the fortune of being educated and well supported. This was not the case in most cases especially in rural areas. Thus was born the Foundation with missionary zeal.

Mirror-Window-Door Approach

As she embarked on this singular mission, she encountered many a hurdles from rural and conservative urban community. She made every parent whose girl child was selected sign a bond that they will ensure that the girl will be allowed to complete the entire education process. This met with stiff opposition from fathers, mothers-in-law and relatives but surprisingly it was mothers who came out in support and insisted on it. Lila found that most mothers were keen that their daughters were not subjected to exploitation they faced.

The *Mirror Approach*, she says, intends to show the *girls what they are and what they are capable of.* The *Window Approach* enables them *to look out and see for themselves what the world has to offer.* The *Door Approach* is intended to *train them with skill sets to enable them walk out and meet the challenges* successfully.

Lila acknowledges but for the environment and people who always rallied around her with support, she could not have made her mark. Her flawless reputation and credibility have been long her steadfast friends. Her success in managing the foundation is an example of how commitment and concern can pave way to sustained results in terms of creating valuable humans. As woman so involved with her career and later with her social work, she makes it clear that a great part of her success would have never been possible without the unflinching support, encouragement at every step and motivation by her husband, Firoz. Managing the home front by balancing the career and family is one quality all women must acquire. She feels that most women are educated but failed to be learned as they have difficulty in adapting, adjusting and accommodating realties of man-woman equations. Women's roles as wife, mother and a daughter-in- law cannot change however much one may wish and that is the truth they need to understand for greater harmony in life. Thus she feels her role extends beyond not just as a provider but also as a mentor to her young girls in enabling them to understand the realities of life. She is a MOM to all of them.

Focus will still remain on the girl child. She has many more miles to go and very many dreams to fulfill. In a world where no matter how much is done, a lot more remains. Issues related to women are still significant. She realizes this and understands that the role she has cut out for herself is not, just a challenge but a passionate commitment she has made to herself. "I believe that you do not have a choice when you get something in life. But what you choose to give, defines you" Optimism all pervasive, she has no doubts on what she wants to do and what she can achieve. *For Lila.... it's her "Tryst with Destiny".*

■ ■ ■

Key Personality Attributes

Face the Reality: At every stage of life, facing reality will mean objectively accepting the reality. This gives strength and direction to find solutions to situations one faces.

Never Let a Challenge Go Unchallenged: To be able to tackle a challenge is a unique quality. Perceiving difficulty as a source motivation to inspire more effort is an important attribute.

Respect and Sensitivity Towards Feelings: Understanding that treating people well is an important ingredient that enables people to contribute.

Dignity and Decorum: Building a personal brand of credibility will be incumbent of a behavior that embodies dignity and decorum.

Single minded Focus: Whatever is on hand must have a single minded focus. Doing things well is more important than doing things simply because they need to be done.

Adjustment and Adaptability: Be it personal or professional life, the key to successful management depends on these two key factors which are the foundation for being or implementing change.

Confidence and Self Motivation: There is no substitute to Self Motivation. Always remember that the best helping hand is at the end of yours.

Ask yourself, "who you are and what you want to do with your life: It does not matter whether you are man or a woman, you are a person who has dreams. Be focused, work hard, have a positive attitude and keep updating skills and knowledge – "That is the only route to success", She says.

Dr. R. A. Mashelakar

To be successful, think different, evaluate your self and reinforce your strengths. Life is all about dreams and working to realize them. Confidence, competence, consistence & persistence are the hall marks of those who race ahead of others.

IN SEARCH OF
AN UNENDING QUEST

Dr. R. A. Mashelakar

A Seed is Nurtured

Epoch making events of life are few and rarely dramatic. When they do happen; the affect may seem innocuous but the impact could be game changing. Invariably such instances shape the thinking, give a new direction to life and spur an enthusiasm which redefines aspirations. A person, an action, an incident or an experience becomes so significant that it changes the whole perspective by revamping the colors of the canvas of future.

The building was far from impressive; typically dilapidated and as expected it was over crowded. The surroundings and infrastructure seemingly under stress and those who patronized, were from a humble background. It was one of the many in the city of Bombay; a municipal school offering free education in Marathi medium and Raghunath was one amongst its students.

Principal Bhave was a man of immense commitment. He taught as if he was possessed; to him teaching was a mission and he taught Physics, Chemistry and Mathematics. He had the art of making his pupils experience science as a practice and not study science on the blackboard. Raghunath, a brilliant student, was drawn to him like a bee to honey.

It was a physics class that day and the topic was convex lens. Principal Bhave while demonstrating the effect of a convex lens by adjusting the distance, began to focus the sun light on to a piece of paper in a narrow beam. As soon as the paper burnt, for some reason he looked directly into the eyes of Raghunath and said "Raghu, life is all about keeping your focus on right things with the right intensity with right consistency and then success is yours". Like an arrow, these words pierced his heart and the impact remained lifelong.

There were many students in that class that day but the incident became a turning point only for Raghunath. Couched in the simplicity of a routine experiment, Principal Bhave ignited a flame of curiosity and inquisitiveness in a young boy who in later years spearheaded India's Science and Technology to unprecedented heights .Thus began an unending affair between Raghunath and science, both becoming symbiotic of each other - insatiable in knowledge and inseparable in quest.

It's a strange phenomenon and occurs world over. A person who does most to shape our lives is always taken for granted; contribution and support is implicit in expectation but acknowledgment is rarely explicit in expression. It's none other than the role Mother's play. Selfless in action and protective in demonstration, a never say die attitude to do good for her child is the universal manifestation of "Mother". For Raghunath, she was not just an embodiment of everything that was human but also everything that was superhuman.

His mother migrated to Bombay, from village Mashel in Goa, after her husband's demise. Raghunath was just six years old. Not educated, with child in tow, out in the wilderness of a city, alone and lonely, she was yet undaunted. It was her mission to see that her child was educated and to enable that, she did not hesitate to put in hard work. Raghunath had little choice regarding education as municipal school was the only means and medium of instruction was vernacular. It would be a euphemism to say that his childhood was challenging and difficult. Growing in this environment, studying outside under the street lights and yet he remained a boy with motivation because his mother was his inspiration. He recalls "I was a brilliant student especially in mathematics, I would always score 100% but occasionally my score would drop to 97% or so. That would never make me unhappy because I would still be the highest in my class but my mother would always ask why I have lost the three marks, her focus was on what was lost implying that the answer to hard work is always perfection not exception". Exception meant that securing 100% is more by default. To her it is implied that 100% effort must lead to 100% result and that is perfection. Perfection to her also meant that it is not a comparison of achievement relative to others but an achievement independent of others. These were important lessons indeed.

"She was my first guru who inculcated the significance of the spirit of excellence at an early age. My basic approach towards, ethics, performance and behavior are her gifts which became my foundation".

Walking the Less Travelled Road

Brilliant as he was, the physical difficulties were kept at bay and he concentrated his energies on excelling in academics. His performance made him eligible for scholarships which sustained him till he completed his education. He had to switch from Marathi medium to English medium post SSC but he never let that hinder his performance since the seeds of excellence were well ingrained. He was selected on merit to IIT Bombay and was also awarded the JRD Tata Meritorious Scholarship which enabled him to complete higher education. He came out of IIT in flying colors and pursued his post graduation in Chemical Engineering which he topped. In those days, it was a convention for all toppers to opt for PhD in a foreign university. Raghunath was offered admission in top universities of USA and Canada. Breaking the convention, to the surprise of all, he chose to pursue PhD under Prof MM Sharma, a 28 years old professor, who had returned from Cambridge and was the youngest at IIT. Raghunath was impressed by his commitment, knowledge, mastery over the subject and infective enthusiasm. The choice was thus made, to pursue PhD under him leaving more prestigious options. Raghunath learnt three very significant things from Prof M M Sharma. Abiding by Professional ethics, value driven mentorship and making best use of constraints.

"The first research paper I wrote was with his assistance, he asked me to credit the authors as "Sharma and Mashlekar", the next research paper written with his support, in which he asked me to credit authors as "Mashelkar and Sharma" giving me the primary credit, the third one was more or less independently done with minimal guidance, he asked me to take the author's credit as "Mashelkar", giving me full acknowledgment for the work. When I asked why he had not put his name, he simply said "this paper was entirely done by you and deserves only your name; If I put my name it will be unethical". Raghunath was stunned because, it was a normal practice by most guides to append their name on all research papers written by their students, irrespective of the fact whether there is any tangible contribution. The second most significant learning was how a strong intention can overcome hurdles in research like minimal research grants. Those days, the research grant Rs 10,000 per year was pale in comparison with around Rs 1,20,000 ($2400) in USA. Though constrained by infrastructure, information and finances, Prof Sharma showed him how intense involvement can find ways and means to overcome these hurdles. Propriety in ensuring credit to researchers and working under deficient conditions imbibed by Raghunath stood by him in years to come. Choosing to join National Chemical laboratory, being part of Council for scientific and Industrial Research, actively choosing a role in evolving and promoting science were actions that signified a spirit that enabled him to choose a less travelled path to address challenges and create solutions.

Experiencing Excellence

Incidents and personal experiences always serve as best lessons in life. Sometimes one experiences and learns and at times someone makes it happen. Raghunath's life too was no exception. His mother's example, Principal Bhave's impression, Prof Sharma's demonstration were impactful.

As a scientist, Raghunath excelled as years passed by. He attained highest positions in the field of science and technology and won innumerable awards and prestigious positions as a man of letters. His contributions in the field of "Scientific Research, Technical and Industrial Research, Leadership and All Round Excellence" led to being appointed as Chair Professor in prestigious Global Universities and on boards of key policy making bodies in India.

One mentor, he acknowledges with great pride, who was instrumental in shaping his scientific approach and enabling a spirit of unending inquisitiveness to seek more is Bharat Ratna Prof (Dr). CNR Rao. He recalls "Dr. CNR Rao is a scientist par excellence. To him its scientific exploration 24x7 that occupies his thoughts. He was much more than a guide and a mentor. At the age of 81, he still works 10 to 12 hours a day, published more than 150 research papers and over 50 books. The energy he displays makes me wonder whether he is 18 or 81 years. Such is his enthusiasm and spirit".

The meeting of Scientific Advisory Board (SAB) to the Prime Minister was in session. SAB is the Apex Advisory Body to the Central Government which formulates, advises and initiates scientific reforms in the country. In chair was the then Prime Minister Rajiv Gandhi. Dr. CNR Rao, the chairman of the SAB was in animated discussion and the Prime Minister was in agreement with his suggestions. As the meeting ended, the Prime Minister asked Dr. Rao to discuss finer details with the Deputy Chairman of Planning Commission (who holds the rank of a cabinet minister) to finalize the details. As soon as the PM departed, the cabinet minister looked at Dr. Rao and in a casual manner told him "Dr. Rao see me in my office tomorrow at 10 am". I was taken aback to see the response of Dr. Rao. In a firm yet a polite tone he replied "Mr. Minister, I hope you know that I am a scientist. I have an experiment in progress in my laboratory tomorrow at Bangalore, which needs my presence and hence I am leaving today. I will inform you once I finish with it and come to meet you". To me, it was a lesson on courage and conviction because it takes more than just courage to take a person of the standing of Deputy Chairman of the Planning Commission. Dr. Rao, could do so not because he was the chairman of SAB, but because of his standing as a scientist of eminence. The minister meekly nodded in agreement and walked out of the chamber.

Raghunath had meteoric rise in the field of science. His work and contributions were acknowledged worldwide. As a natural outcome of his intellectual contributions, he became the first Indian to earn very prestigious nominations in Science and technology. Nomination as the Fellow of Royal Society of Science UK was the first major milestone in his career. Raghunath felt quite elated and proud of this fact and went to Dr. CNR Rao to tell him about his achievement. He anticipated an enthusiastic response and appreciation; however, Dr. Rao looked up and simply nodded an acknowledgment with nothing said in praise. Raghunath felt a pang of disappointment but accepted it gracefully.

Nomination as the Fellow of US National Academy of Science was the next feather in his cap. This achievement in reality was the ultimate; only next to the Nobel Prize. Established in 1780 by Benjamin Franklin, it had the likes of Charles Darwin, Albert Einstein and Winston Churchill on its Roll of Honor. Since then, only six Indians received this honor and Raghunath was the seventh and the first one as an engineer. As Raghunath informed his mentor, with excitement and expectation, the scene he encountered was similar. The response was lukewarm and his mentor hardly showed any signs of pleasure or appreciation and just a token acknowledgment was forthcoming. Raghunath was justifiably hurt and felt disappointed and could no longer control his anguish.

"Sir, I have achieved such significant milestones but received no appreciation from you; please tell what is that I should do to impress you"?

Dr. CNR Rao looked at him with a most benevolent expression and said, "Raghu, I want you to remember that you are a scientist. For a scientist there is just one ladder of excellence and which adds one step with every step you climb. There is no limit to scientific excellence. I am of course very proud of you but I don't want you to think that you have ascended the ladder of excellence because that would be the beginning of the end to an inquisitive mind". For Raghunath this was a reinforcement of what his mother had said in his school days. Persistence, focus and attention, exceptional leadership and courage and pursuit of excellence are the lessons, Raghunath would attribute to Dr. CNR Rao.

Evolving Relationships: People - Technology – Industry – Governance

Raghnath is a firm believer in technology and its role as a force multiplier in enabling better growth and living. When asked by Barack Obama, President of USA, at a formal introduction as to what he does with science, Raghunath replied "Sir, I make science work for the common man". In today's evolving world, science and technology have a tremendous role; the shift in thinking from *Knowledge is wealth to Knowledge only can create wealth*" is significantly true. The relationship between industry and commerce is fast becoming knowledge sensitive and thus enabling innovation to be more and more relevant.

India achieved political independence in 1947; Economic independence in 1990's; Technology access around 2008. From supply centric economy devoid of choice to the customer, there is a transformation to demand driven economy with customer sensitive environment. Competition and competitiveness have added a challenge to business models shifting focus from product and price to variety, quality, accessibility and affordability. It is here that science and technology play a major role and innovation in research becomes immensely relevant.

Raghnath illustrates with a case in point; just a decade prior India had hardly 15 million mobile phones; Today India has over 95 million. The three A's *"Acceptability, Accessibility and Affordability"* became the foundation for success. A handset costing $250 is now available for $25. In India, if mobiles were to proliferate reduction in call rates was inevitable from 10 cents per minute to below one cent per minute. The companies had to reinvent themselves by drastically dropping call prices and giving flexible options for the customer. Today, India presents a gloriously diverse picture of a roadside sweeper and an affluent businessman in a Mercedes Benz being in position to access the mobile and its benefits due to innovation in communication.

Innovation Vs Jugaad or Mind Vs Mindset

Raghunath is full of passion when it comes to making contributions that enable a positive change. There is a gleam in his eyes and fervor in his voice when he talks about how he wishes to see India as a technology leader of tomorrow. The biggest challenge is that education and technology are addressing more of mind and less on changing the mind set. He illustrates by saying "People are willing to accept the new technology of an Apple i 6; that's the mind but in the same vein refuse to accept a girl in marriage if she is manglik (A zodic sign considered unauspicious for girls); that's the mindset. We have sent a Mission to Mars and have demonstrated the capability of mind but many of whom who are part of this Mangalyan technology mission would still hesitate to accept a girl who is a manglik", This simple explanation is the seat of deep rooted malaise which technology and education must address.

The Indian mindset with respect to accepting technology also needs to shift from jugaad mentality of make do mindset. Raghunath says "Innovation focuses on alternatives, solutions and empowerment through use of technology where as Jugaad is a state of mind which relies on quick fix without any relevance to quality, safety or permanence of solution". Here too, it is a conflict between mind and the mind set. The use of mind leads to a Jugaad mentality and change of mindset will result in creating innovations.

How things have changed and why innovation is relevant can be understood the way healthcare has evolved in the past few decades. First it was Preventive care with use of vaccines, then came curative care with use of antibiotics, the next was Predictive care involving Genomes and gene therapy and now its regenerative care with innovation in regenerating organs like liver, kidney etc. Such changes and many more have become relevant because of the changing needs of the society calling for greater innovative use of technology. In India, though science and scientific research are on the rise, the issue of aggressively targeting mindsets remains a challenge.

The Long Walk Ahead

Though the journey ahead is long, Raghunath feels India is destined to be the destination of future. He attributes three important advantages that favor India's evolution amongst nations of the world. "To my mind Demography, Diversity and Democracy are the three pillars of future. The fact that we are the youngest nation with more than 55% of the population below 25 years of age augurs well because they are ready to seek challenges and make innovations. Democracy is our foundation which will encourage free thinking and in years to come we mature to become more vibrant and better governed and lastly, Divergence is the foundation of innovation since the needs of a diverse society are numerous and pose an intellectual challenge. A mono culture is a hindrance to innovative thinking.

Come what may; Raghunath is firm in his resolve. He will and he shall continue his scientific endeavors to contribute and promote science and technology for the well being of the common man. For him there is no end to the beginnings he makes and he remains as always "In search of an Unending Quest".

■ ■ ■

Key Learning Values

Effort Never Ceases: Effort never dies because it can never cease. The requirement is to continuously commit oneself through lifelong learning.

Persistence: Success is a long term perspective and invariably requires persistent approach to tackle ups and downs.

Identify and Pursue Passion: Effort and persistence are interconnected with in passion. It is significant for those who wish seek a career first identify what they wish to pursue. Absence of passion can prove disastrous in the long run.

Competing with Self: While comparison and bench marking may be relevant, it is necessary to push one to own limits of capability. Many times comparisons may lead to inadequate conclusions

Confidence and Self Belief: Most battles are lost because people give up believing that they do not possess the requisite capabilities like English medium education, blue chip background etc. Self confidence and belief can overcome any such hurdles.

Shared Values of Life: It is very important to imbibe, demonstrate and propagate shared value systems. These are the foundation for credibility.

Dr. V. D. Karad

Circumstances however challenging can be overcome if competency exists. To pursue a mission all one need is a dream with determination drive and diligence to sustain.

ON AN EXTRAORDINARY UNRELENTING MISSION

Dr. V. D. Karad

Exceptional Exception

As the Sholapur bound train leaves the limits of Pune city, the passengers are exposed to an unexpected spectacle. Springing out of nowhere, as though designed by the hand of God, a unique landscape unveils itself.

Under the glow of the setting sun spreading over the pristine beauty of an architectural wonder; an observer is awe stuck. The experience of the passing view is compelling, inspiring, elevating and in a way intriguing. Compelling because of the beauty and design, inspiring because the sight touches the heart and comforts the mind, elevating because of its unique aesthetics and visual harmony and intriguing because it makes one wonder as to whose brainchild could it be to create such an invoking place.

This campus, known as Rajbagh, is one of the many which have come up to represent value, integrity and quality in education, MIT represents.

Maharashtra Institute of Technology, a constituent of Maharashtra Academy of Engineering Education and Research, (MAEER) an educational trust, spread across many campuses in Kothrud, Loni, Alandi, Pandharpur, Latur and Talegaon. MAEER Trust represents a phenomenal achievement. In a short span of over 30 years, it has grown exponentially from a single engineering college to a multi disciplinary academic giant integrating most domains and managing over 60 institutions from, KG to PG.

Every achievement of this nature is an outcome of passionate commitment and such involvement usually manifests itself with a missionary zeal. To such a person, difficulties do not matter, hurdles never obstruct, resources do not hinder and motivation never ceases. Dr. Vishwanth Dadarao Karad, with never ending ardor and energy has been instrumental in shaping the destiny of MAEER and creating an institution which has embedded itself in the modern contemporary history of Pune with a unique imprint.

Beyond the Ordinary

Destiny often reveals its hand with many surprises in store. How the journey of life gets scripted and the manner in which one evolves is always a matter of intrigue. Vishwanth was born in a small village called Rameshwar Rui in Latur district of Maharashtra. His father Dadarao Karad was a pious man and a strict follower of Warkari (A religious movement within the spiritual tradition of Hinduism) traditions and Vaishanav (one of the major branches of Hinduism focused on veneration of Lord Vishnu) Sampradaya (Conventions). He was brought up in very austere living conditions and the family ambience was embedded with rich culture, tradition and value systems based on a high code of conduct and ethics. Rameshwar was small village having a population of around 1500 people. The village was no different from others with hardly any worthwhile infrastructure to boast about. There was no electricity, no water connection; the roads were dusty tracks, very minimal medical care and there was no school.

An adhoc school was run by Venkat Rao Kulkarni, who informally took upon himself the responsibility of giving basic education up to class IV to the children of the village and Vishwanath was one of his students. There was no place to teach as such and the cowshed served as their classroom.

The children assembled daily in his cowshed, after the cattle were sent out for the day. It was their responsibility to clean, sweep, swab and maintain the area before the commencement of the class. Venkat Rao was a passionate teacher and he made up for the lack of facilities with his teachings. As the evening approached, the children would eagerly wait for sound of the bells hanging from the neck of the cows returning back, as this meant the day's school was over. In such circumstances, began the education of Vishwanath; no books or texts, no chairs and tables, no classroom with basic comforts and learning in local language.

It is possibly because of this, he remained rooted to the belief that humility and humbleness as the basic traits that define a person and never to pre judge people. This experience made him realize that if competency exists and is supported by hard work; circumstances do not hinder but accelerate growth.

As a child, Vishwanath was a regular visitor to the Samadhi of Gopal Maharaj, a well known saint. He recalls "I always used to ask for three things; firstly, I would seek his blessings that I should be granted "Satbudhi"(Good sense to think good about people), secondly, I would ask him to ensure that I do no harm to any one and lastly, a personal wish, to make me come first in my class".

For a person not blessed with a silver spoon, difficulties and hurdles become a part and parcel at every stage of life. Since Rameshwar had no structured school, he was sent to a boarding at a small town called Madha, located 140 kms from his village. At Madha, the boarding was run by Ganpat Rao Sathe. He was doing this to support children from poor families like Vishwanth to enable them to complete their schooling. There were many who could not afford to pay and Vishwanath was paying a "princely" sum of Rs 5 per month towards everything. Life was quite tough; comforts were very minimal thus Vishwanath had to fend for himself in many ways as money was limited. Since the boarding had to look after a lot of children, the food was very simple. In order to feed the children, Ganpat Rao would procure Milo (Low quality Jowar-Sorgham), sent to India by USA under PL (Public Law) 480 aid to underdeveloped countries which was very cheap. Using this jowar, Bhakri (A round flat unleavened bread) was made and it was served with thin vegetable gravy made out of discarded green chilies and vegetables collected from the market. Vishwanth recollects "It may sound unbelievable, but to us hungry boys, this was a heavenly dish. I can recollect the tangy taste of the meal even today and can say with pleasure that eating that meal was more satisfying and enjoyable than eating a meal at the five star Taj Mahal Hotel in Mumbai"

For those who thrive through challenges, difficulties are meant to be overcome. Vishwanth was one of those who possibly thrived in difficulties. A quality which emerged very early in life. His highly commendable academic record is a testimony of this fact. He passed S.S.C. Examination in 1958 in First Class with Distinction, stood first in the school and second in Sholapur Center. His excellent academic career in school and HSC changed the course of his ambition of joining the non technical stream and become a collector to shifting over to the technical stream to join engineering. Those days engineering colleges in Maharashtra were very few and getting admission in engineering college at Pune was a very significant achievement which was only possible for brilliant students. Very significant occurrences in life emerge out of seemingly insignificant happenings. One such event happened with Vishwanath which made a huge impact on his life, direction, focus and aspirations.

During the first year, he found a small booklet on Swami Vivekananda. Out of sheer curiosity, he read that book. The impact was profound. He read and re-read and soon realized the import of the teachings of Swami Vivekananda and became his ardent disciple and made a resolve to pursue his teachings and propagate them for the larger good of the society. This imprint on an impressionable mind would determine the future and mission of Vishwanth.

On completion of BE (Mechanical Engineering), he pursued his post graduation and completed ME (Mechanical). This enabled him to secure a job as lecturer in College of Engineering Pune and thus began his career as a teacher of distinction.

Extraordinarily True Legend

Some incidents of life seem to be legendary. Stories of courage, dedication and sacrifice are often found in the chronicles of history but the story of Prayag Akka is beyond an extraordinary legend. Extraordinary because it's something outside the capacity of an ordinary mortal to achieve and legendary because of its iconic nature.

Vishwanath was rather young when his mother passed away. The family was large with three brothers and four sisters. Prayag Akka was the eldest, around twenty years of age, was newly married and on the threshold of starting her new life. The family was in a state of shock and grief. Being from a traditional Vaishnav Sampraday, the last rites were conducted with due regards and in conformity with Hindu traditions.

On the tenth day, the Pind (An offering of rice balls cooked on firewood) ceremony was in progress. The congregation had all the close relatives and the family. On conclusion of the ceremony, the priest laid out the balls of rice at the designated place. As per the Hindu traditions, once the Pind is laid out by the priests, it is supposed to be consumed by crows. The eating of rice balls by the crows is symbolic of the fact that the soul of the person who passed away is content and fully at rest. Usually, a host of crows would sweep down and devour the rice balls and on that day there were a large flock of crows; all of them sitting around the offering but none consuming. This was indicative of the fact that the soul was dissatisfied or worried. Anticipating that the source of concern as the well being of the children, Vishawanth's father bowed down and promised to take care of the children but to no avail; the family and relatives too made a solemn promise to ensure the children are cared for, still nothing happened and it became a source of concern as the Pind was still untouched. As deliberations were on, Prayag Akka suddenly got up and went to the pyre. She took the ashes in her hands and wiped off the sindhoor (traditional red or orange red color cosmetic powder worn by married woman on the forehead along parting of the hair) from her forehead to the shock of all those present. Wiping off the sindhoor in Hindu custom symbolized widowhood and Prayg Akka was recently married. She applied ashes on her arms and then declared that she has opted to take Sanyas (Path of Renunciation) from that moment and would dedicate herself to the family and her brothers and sisters and promised to look after them till her last breath. She looked at her husband and announced that she has freed him from the wedlock and he can remarry and restart his life once again. At that instant, the unbelievable happened; crows swooped down in hordes and ate away the pind. Since that day till the day she passed away, Prayag Akka remained with the family taking care of every need of every family member, living in austerity and having just one meal a day.

Vishwanth attributes his success and the well being of the entire family to the unrelenting effort, supreme sacrifice and the blessings of Prayag Akka. This incident had an indelible impression on Vishwanath and he always considered her as his mother and elevated her to the status of a deity in his mind.

Ideas and Ideals

Vishwanath is a man of ideas and ideals. It is this innovative quest in him that led to creation of numerous institutions and propagating ideas and concepts many may never dare to venture. He believes that if the intent is good and the commitment is total, there will always be a way to any issue. During his days as Assistant Professor at College of Engineering, he wrote a monumental article which actually changed the face of private education in professional courses in Maharashtra. It was early 1980's, those days Maharashtra did not permit private colleges to run engineering courses. As a result, the number of seats were very limited and many students from Maharashtra had to go to other states to study engineering due to lack of opportunity. Vishwanath made out a strong case for privatization of engineering colleges and wrote an article in newspapers which attracted wide debate and the attention of then Chief Minister Vasantdada Patil. Impressed by the logic and accepting the need, the Chief Minister soon put in place the necessary changes in policy thus enabling establishment of private engineering colleges. The Chief Minister also invited Vishwanth to establish an Engineering college and granted him permission to do so.

Vishwanth was a college professor with meager resources. He neither had the land nor the money to start an engineering college. He was required to pay sum of Rs 40000, a very substantial amount those days to the government as a fee to get the approval. "I really had no choice except to surrender this offer given to me. Suddenly I came to know of Dr. Subhash Ghaisas, who owned a plot of land at Kothrud and I decided to approach him". He had no earlier acquaintance with Dr. Ghaisas; as he waited in his clinic he began to wonder if this will work. When called, Vishwanth discussed the proposal and frankly requested him to give his land for establishing the first private engineering college. Dr. Ghaisas after hearing the proposal simply accepted the same and gave him 15 acres of land on which MIT stands proudly today.

What started as a trickle became a flood. In a short span of 30 years or so, MIT has scaled phenomenal heights and has acquired a reputation for values, traditions and quality education. It became probably the first institution to introduce uniforms for engineering students and subsequently for all disciplines to ensure uniformity and decorum. MIT banned smoking on campus three decades ago well before the current rules in this regard. MIT also maintains itself as pure vegetarian campus. Today, there are more than 60 inter disciplinary institutions spread across five campuses offering education to nearly 60000 students across India and abroad.

Vishwanth also took up the issues relating to Indian culture and traditions passionately. The book which stirred his conscience as a student in first year of engineering was still in his heart and words spoken by Swami Vivekananda still resonated within. He became a firm believer and took upon himself the challenge of dispelling the uninformed belief amongst most Indians that everything our saints spoke was religion and not philosophy. The words of Vivekananda "Union of science, religion/spirituality alone can bring peace and harmony to mankind" became a dictum which he ardently started to propagate.

He established the World Peace Centre and on the lines of the conference attended by Vivekananda in 1833, he conducted the World Philosophers Meet in Pune. He was successful in convincing the world philosophers that saints like Tukaram and Dyneshwar were not religious leaders but philosophers and their writings were nothing but exposition of natural laws of science and living. He also expounded the fact that Albert Einstein's revelation "Oh! God, now I realize that the entire universe is a manifestation of pure consciousness" is same as what Dyneshwara said in the very first page of Dyneshwari more than 800 years ago.

His commitment to education, extension and propagation of traditional values and culture, contribution towards peace through tolerance and integration of religions earned him a rare honor of being bestowed UNESCO Chair, the first in Asia. The milestones achieved by Vishwanth were astounding. He attributes all this to two factors. The first, blessings, sacrifice and prayers of Pragya Akka and secondly, to sincerity in effort and commitment with integrity.

Not once but many a times in this journey, help and assistance came in large quantum from unknown people who placed implicit faith and trust. What is it that made them do so; He says "I have always been transparent, truthful and fully committed to whatever I wanted to do. I think when people observe these qualities, they tend to repose trust. How else one can explain the family of Raj Kapoor handing over such large tracts of prime land to me for developing infrastructure for education. If sincerity and truthfulness are demonstrated, people come forward to help." He also believes sanctity of intent and desire to do good to others is an important factor that begets trust.

While education through Indian values has been a constant drive for Vishwanath, the other area which he has his heart fully committed is propagation of the real meaning of the teachings of Vivekananda, Sant Tukaram and Dyneshwar Mauli. He feels pained that people out of sheer ignorance are unable to distinguish between "Shardha (Faith)" and "Andha Shradha (Superstition/Blind faith)". To him, it is exasperating to perceive, how the scientific interpretation of universal laws of nature in our scriptures has been misrepresented as religious discourse. This has been so strongly enforced in the Indian mindset that we tend to believe this more than the truth. Propagating this truth has become a missionary zeal and he pursues this with endearing enthusiasm. To Vishwanth, being Indian and respecting Indian values, culture and ethos is more important and it is this fervour which drives him to consistently undertake actions to emphasize these expectations.

He believes the words of Swami Vivekananda that "this is the century of India and it will show the path of peace and prosperity to the world".

The trends are already visible and Vishwanth feels that people like him must commit themselves more to sensitize the younger generation to understand and take pride in Indian values and culture. He wants the younger generation to be "Physically strong, Mentally robust, Emotionally balanced and Spiritually elevated". This he feels can only be achieved if we can create an awareness of Sampradaya (Philosophy of tradition), accepted with Nishta (Loyalty), executed with Shradha (Dedication), enabling acquisition of Vigyaan (Knowledge), ensuring Samrudhi (Adequacy), leading to Sukh (Sense of happiness and harmony) and finally enabling Shanti (Peace within) .

To Vishwanath, this is not a dream because he believes everything starts from self and thus, his mission is to pursue this vision and promote and embed these thoughts in young minds, to shape the future of tomorrow. He is indeed "On an Extraordinary Unrelenting Mission" undeterred and unmindful; with positive hopes for a prosperous and peaceful India.

■ ■ ■

<u>Key Learning Values</u>

Never to be Daunted by Difficulty: Challenges and difficulties in life must be faced with belief and confidence. Every difficulty has a solution and every solution is achievable.

Persevere with Belief: A strong sense of faith in what one believes as ideals is very essential to set a direction for life.

Learning to Share: Life is all about sharing; whether it is what we earn or what we learn - the true value for life is only when it is shared.

Humbleness and Humility: Irrespective of the level of success, one must be rooted to reality. Every step one climbs is always because support and hence learning to be humble and displaying humility in the face of praise is very essential.

Communication with Commitment: The value of communication is determined by its credibility. Credibility is demonstration in action of words spoken. It therefore very important to communicate only what one can actually commit.

Passion for Mission: Life is all about pursuing one's mission. Every mission which is important to an individual must be taken up with passion. Action without mission and passion ends up as a day dream.

D. S. Kulkarni

Success is never instant. It needs perseverance, patience and more importantly "a goodness of purpose".

AN ARCHITECT OF OWN DREAMS

D. S. Kulkarni

Impressionable Impressions

In fact, there was no summer. Year around, the climate in Pune was very congenial. For nine months one would experience a combination of monsoon and winter, the remainder three, a blend of summer and spring with hardly a semblance of heat we experience today. The traffic was minimal, the rivers were perennial, flowing with fresh water, good enough for young boys to plunge into and swim; trees abounded everywhere and by sunset, the city was a picture of quaint placid ambience. Under the dim lights of the street falling into the courtyard, a group of ladies were assembling for an evening ritual. As a daily routine, the house wives of the Wada (residential area with shared amenities) in Kasbapeth, would meet after completing their household chores for social interaction. It was an informal meeting to share their experiences of the day and spend an hour together before they would wind back to their homes. Young Dilip was around; his mother was holding the ladies attention. She was explaining to others the reasons which prompted her leave her job to start her own small "Aanganwadi School". (Courtyard School) "I had to take my youngest son to the school where I worked as a housekeeper. My job entailed cleaning of the school, classrooms, offices and toilets. At times, I had to attend to him whenever he cried but I was very particular and would take pains by working extra to complete my work. One day, the Principal shouted and humiliated me by remarking that my child was a nuisance and I cannot attend to him at work. He told me in no uncertain terms that either I stop bringing the child or quit the job. I was hurt because I never ever used the pretext of my child for abstaining from work and was annoyed because, I felt that I was being pressurized because I was helpless and in need. I told him, that I will not leave my child at home and indignantly retorted that I will start my own school. I quit working the very same day. The incident made me resolve that I need do something on my own to earn with respect and thus was born the Balvikas Mandir. To earn a living while helping other mothers escape the agony I faced." As the ladies clapped in appreciation, Dilip's young heart was filled with a sense of pride. The story made a distinct impression on his young mind for three reasons. Firstly, His mother's fearless self confidence in taking on the challenge in spite of being a third standard pass with no formal qualification. Secondly, she had the courage and conviction to stand up to an issue she believed was right and thirdly, her example of never compromising self respect. The impact of this impression would be perceptible in Dilip in days to come. Dilip Recalls "I was born in a rich family... We never had money the way rich had but we never felt the need because we were rich in values. To me, it's not feeling the need; its absence of craving for more which is the hallmark of richness of life".

It was in effect, a cultured lower middle class family, his father was a Police Constable and mother a multi faceted personality, housewife, school housekeeper, Aanganwadi teacher, tutor, expert draper and guide to other ladies in the Wada. The environment in which he grew up had a distinct culture and lifestyle manifested by emotional bonding coming from collaborative living. He grew up a happy child with very little needs, in an environment that was blended with trust, confidence and belief in goodness of sharing. There was a tremendous amount of emotional support from everyone within and beyond the family. He recalls "In Wada culture, everybody was family. If guests who come on a visit find that the hosts were away, the neighbor's would look after them as their own. If a child does not return home in time after sunset, it was assumed that the child is at neighboring Joshi Kaka's (Uncle) home. If he does not turn up for dinner, parents' would think the child was having dinner there and if he still does not return, parents would be assured that the child must have fallen asleep on the lap of the grandmother listening to her stories. Unlike today, where tensions are prevalent and trust is at deficit: those days were golden days of living together in harmony."

Observing What Others Fail to See

From a very early age, Dilip decided to be on his own. He had his own mind, took a lot of decisions and even started to earn his own money. He was fiercely independent, eager and restless. Some traits always manifest early and these were the early indicators of future.

Those days, they would come back from school early afternoon and there after his friends were expected to help their father's in their respective occupational activity. Since both parents were employed, Dilip was the only one who was free. All his friends had to complete their work before they could join for play. Many a times they would seek his help and Dilip took upon him to assist them in completing various chores.

Babban Gote needed help as his father operated a "tonga" (horse drawn cart for conveyance) . He had to clean the shed, massage and wash the horse and then feed him, before he could be spared. Dilip took up this work to help him a number of times and learnt the art of handling the horse. Pardesi needed help in operating the snack Kiosk of his father which sold "Spiced Chana" (Bengal gram), he would chip in for his friend and very soon started operating independently to realize that he was earning much more than the competitors in the area. Ganesh needed help at Amuratalya, a small hotel run by his father and here too Dilip assisted by washing dishes, wiping the tables, laying out utensils and keeping the area clean. Bharat Rathore needed help in packing supari satchets to be made ready for sale in the market.

Each of these chores gave important lessons to Dilip... while washing and massaging the horse, he experienced the sheer joy of kindness through the eyes of the horse which conveyed silent affection; He realized the importance of competition and how to get better of it by better service, variety and presentation at the snack stall as customers preferred him because he presented himself very neatly and organized the kiosk very efficiently with better variety; At the hotel, he understood the importance of cleanliness and hygiene and how customers perceived it as a measure of quality, reliability and trust: while packing the supari satchets he learnt to be honest and committed to ensuring correct quantity and right quality of supari.

Keen observation coupled with hands on work bestowed an understanding at a very young age that many may never learn in their lifetime. Inadvertently, he grasped the essentials of business strategy by understanding how to get better of competition, realized the need for product differentiation and correct customer segmentation, understood the importance of empathy and importance of quality and trust because "he observed what others failed to see."

Work is Respect and Self Respect

"How does one do business" he asked "When you have No Money, No Qualification, No Background and No Resources"? With the God given hands if one pursues any job with conviction, commitment and integrity, success will chase you" and that's the belief he nurtured and the belief he followed. The proof is the way his life unfolded. His first earning came from selling the newspapers on the day SSC Board results were declared. On his bicycle, he sold these papers at a premium and earned a princely sum of Rs 80. To earn money to meet his own expenses, he left no stone unturned. This he did not because he needed money, but because he wanted to be independent and find ways to be creative and earn in an honest way. His first job was with Dhamankar, a newspaper distributor. Every day he was required to report at 5:45 AM for collection of papers. One day, he was late and reached the place at 6 AM. Dhamankar looked at him as he came closer and gave him a tight slap and asked him to leave. The slap shook Dilip, and he decided to quit the job. He recalls "I left primarily because I felt humiliated by the slap and decided that in future, I will never work for anyone". Later, I realized, more as an after thought, the importance of punctuality as the customers expect newspapers at a particular time and even a minute's delay makes them highly dissatisfied. This incident is a major turning point because it shaped the entire future and thinking of Dilip and gave new direction to his life. It made him think of ways and means to look for opportunities for business while giving him the understanding of respecting the self respect of subordinates and adherence to discipline and delivery.

He never hesitated to work, anything anytime as long as it was honest and rewarding. One experience he recalls while working at the vegetable shop. "One day, a lady came to our vegetable cart. I was helping the owner. As he started to weigh her vegetables on the weighing scale, she asked him to stop and wanted me to weigh it for her. On inquiry by the surprised owner, she said, the tilt of the weighing scale is always towards the customer when I weighed and thus it was more accurate". This incident, made Dilip realize the need to think the customers way did and satisfy them, by giving a bit more. This "A Little Bit More" philosophy came very much in handy in the later years when handling customers and employees at Toyota dealerships.

He completed his schooling and passed his higher secondary examinations without any difficulty. He was not an outstanding student but he never failed either. Passing in one go was an achievement those days and the rat race for marks was non existent.

Moment of Joy

Diwali was around the corner; A festival of lights which brings in a lot of delight. As a practice, his father would usually buy one packet of crackers worth Rs 5 every year for the entire family. Resources were meager and his parents main concern was to make their children's life comfortable. Dilip was busy at work that year and had a substantial saving. He went up to his father and gave him his entire earning of Rs 22 and requested his father to buy crackers, sweets and clothes for all.

It was moment so finely etched in Dilip's memory. Scene was emotional though no words were spoken, he recollects the expression of pride and the tinge of moisture in his father's eye; the affectionate pat and a wordless acknowledgement said it all. "It's still the happiest moment of my life" he recalls with joy and pleasure.

From cleaning of telephones, washing shop boards, distributing papers, selling vegetables, selling second hand books, lottery tickets, starting a business of scent for use in telephones: There was no work which was menial and everything he did was with sincerity and diligence, pleasing his customers with courtesy, demonstrating good manners and behavior, Dilip learnt the ropes of business, the hard way. His parents never asked him to work, but at the same time never discouraged him as they firmly believed Work is worship and the true message of respecting value of work rather than value for work was given to him at an early age.

Earning to Live Not Living to Earn

Dilip today presides over a massive multi crore empire spanning across segments like Real Estate, Automobile, Education, Technology, Social work, all built on an edifice of unblemished reputation. He is the brand and the company's reputation is measured by his personal standing. The real lesson on the importance of establishing personal credibility and trust came to him by Prof. Vasant Nurkar, Principal, Ness Wadia College. He is the one who supported him during his college by permitting him to continue with his business. When he needed an investment of Rs 500, he took him to the bank and stood as his guarantor. That day, Prof Nurkar told him "This loan is given to you on trust. Remember never to default and never lose this trust. Once you establish this, you will get not Rs 500 but Rs 5 lakhs because people will trust you". This lesson left a telling effect and Dilip says with pride in all these decades of business there has never been a case of default and today banks queue up for giving loans. He associates his liberal thinking to his fortune of having spent a childhood in emotionally strengthening circumstances, support from his family for his ventures, ability to respect work and the worker and attributes like empathy, larger sense of well being for all and disciplined way of life and business. His mother's lesson on making a living while making others happy, led to his firm belief that earning must lead to enhancement of living of all who contribute towards it.

A "Ghati" Businessman.

It sounds incredulous but true; that's what many called him for his commitment to a business model which is so unlike a viable business. Can a business be sound where against a turnover of over Rs 100 Crores, the outcome in terms of profit is mere Rs 1.5 crores? Would any businessman with eye for profit continue to pursue such a business with unbridled enthusiasm? The business in question was the Toyota Dealership. A passion that has become a business for Dilip. A total of 13 dealerships, employing over 3500 people with an investment of over

Rs 120 crores, DSK Toyota has been a symbol of success. Excellence in performance and customer relations have been instrumental in enabling DSK to be the winner of "Best Dealership Awards" globally over the last decade. Dilip recalls with pride his Toyota Journey because it not just about being the best, its more about the culture of citizenship that has been created in the hearts of all employees. They feel they own, they care and they contribute because they are well looked after. He says, "All my dealer establishments are located in prime locations on land varying from 2 to 5 acres. If I sell my business and dispose off my land, I can easily raise Rs 500 crores and by investing it in a fixed deposit in State Bank of India, I can earn an annual interest of 40 crores. After tax deduction, I will earn around Rs 25 crores annually which would be more than 15 times the profit I earn. But will that give me the happiness that I have today? 3500 employees depend on me and I look after them well: they are paid well, they own a house, send their children to good schools, most of them own cars and have excellent medical support in top hospitals. It is their smile that brings value to my business and adds purpose to my life" The impact of the earliest lesson he learnt hearing his mother's story finds its semblance here.

After Thoughts

Happiness and Success, Dilip, feels are not synonymous of money or profit earned. Everything must have an objective that goes beyond. Recalling his moment of life when he felt he was the richest, he says "The day I sold the newspapers announcing SSC results, both my pockets were full of coins. I earned Rs 80 that day. As I stood with my palms filled with coins; I felt I was the richest man on the earth. Not withstanding the multi crore assets today, I still feel I was richest that day".

For a man who scripted his own life, his firm belief has been to seek out opportunities, to be an opportunist from the perspective of seizing the right one. He says "Opportunity does not come with an appointment;

one has to be aware and be ready for it". To look at what has been gained rather than what has been lost will give an outlook of positivity and propel one towards success with satisfaction. A never say die approach, willingness to work hard and work with own hands in any capacity, in any job, believing in integrity of work and value addition and giving out the best with a passion for sharing the good for the well begin of all, will always result in a successful life".

Coming from a man who walked the talk by being what he says, these are indeed words that inspire belief that success is never instant and one needs perseverance and patience with goodness of purpose.

Dilip looks much beyond, he has an unfinished agenda, age is still too far to catch up and his enthusiasm has an effusive effect. Like a sculptor, he continues to chisel and remains an "architect of his own dreams." He stands truly tall amongst many who rose and will remain tall amongst many who will rise in future... The story goes on.

■ ■ ■

Key Personality Attributes

Respect for Work: It does not matter what type of work that is needed to be done as long as it is honest and rewarding.

Observing and Learning: Most people become passengers in life as they pass through their lives without observing and thus never learning. Keen and astute sense of observation is the key to success.

Agility in Seizing Opportunity: Opportunities never announce their arrival. Mental agility is a must to make the best of fleeting opportunities.

Need for Value Addition: Every customer expects value addition. Providing service is an expectation and giving value addition is excellence.

Learning the Hard Way: There is no way other than learning by working the hard way. Best experiences are the ones, that are learnt by own experience.

Evolving Brand value through Integrity and Commitment: Best brand is the acknowledgement of customers who consider you trustworthy. There are thus no short cuts to branding.

Combining Social Well Being with Business Objective: Its essential to have a larger perspective of business. Success must pave way for satisfaction.

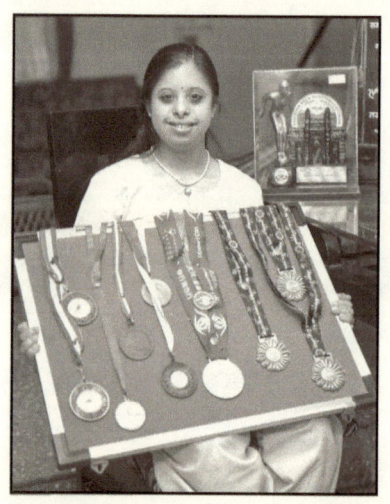

Gauri Gadgil

In life, accepting things that cannot change is important to find effective alternatives. "Accept first, act next and sustain throughout" should be the credo.

TOGETHER FOREVER: A BINDING BOND

Sneha & Gauri Gadgil

A Startling Occurence

In Central India, it's a chilly winter and December 1990 was no exception. Sneha was blissfully enjoying her new found status of a "mother to be". The way it happens in most Indian households, she was at her parents place for her first delivery. For a young girl, soon to be mother, these were amazing times. A fine sense of anticipation, a feeling of exhilaration, a bit of apprehension coupled with the fear of the unknown and a tingling tinge of happiness, all coming together blending into a unique emotional experience. This was also the time for expectations, as mothers would conjuncture on multiple possibilities and near ones would rally around to give as much comfort and affection to enable this memorable transition. It's in such an environment, amidst a resurgent mood; a tremendous feeling of being someone special seems to have embraced Sneha. Her stay at her paternal home was in every way comfortable and she was well cared for under the watchful eyes of her mother and protective shoulder of her father. It seemed all was well set, still two more months to go she thought and was hopeful of an unfettered outcome.

As the day progressed, a sudden discomfiture started setting in, within a short span of time it became evident that something serious was afoot as Sneha was distinctly uncomfortable. Her parents rushed her to the hospital. She went through an early labor and thus was born her first child; a baby girl, eight weeks ahead of time. It was obvious that the childbirth was complicated, the doctors managed a safe delivery but there were many problems to address. Grossly underweight, afflicted with jaundice (which lasted for 2 months), the baby was in intensive care undergoing UV treatment and was on life support. To make matters difficult, she was diagnosed with "Down's Syndrome (Trisomy-A Genetic disorder by birth)" a permanent congenital (something which occurs by birth) disorder which effects the child's natural development.

Destiny in its inexplicable way, made the most unexpected happen, leaving Sneha in distress as it dawned on her that her little baby who was so tenaciously fighting to survive would be a special child and differently abled for life!

Momentous Moments

It was Shanghai, China, which was hosting the Special Olympics Summer Games in October 2007. Gauri, the girl who started her life with a tenacity to survive and a will to win, was one of the contenders in the 50m Butterfly stroke. The event was over and the time was set for the distribution of medals.

Standing under the shadow of the Indian flag with pride, was Gauri. As she stepped forward, on hearing the announcer call her name to acknowledge specially the performance of Gauri, who came a very close fourth position, Sneha was overwhelmed. She could do little to stop tears rolling down her cheeks; these were tears of pent up emotions, of trials and tribulations, of difficulties and deadlocks. It was the final vindication of her untiring effort and affection. Seeing her little girl oblivious of what she had achieved but beaming with happiness at that moment of acknowledgement, the sense of achievement and satisfaction was beyond words to express.

She recalled, "When things like this happen, one tends to introspect. It's not about how much was achieved but it's all about how much we believed we could. It is this singular purpose which drove both of us to take up challenges that came our way".

Gauri who transformed herself from the nondescript entity of a specially abled child to a celebrity for having achieved laurels not just in sports but also in cinema, has indeed come a long long way.

The Arduous Journey

It was very difficult for Sneha and her family to face the truth. She recalls "I was upset and dejected as any mother would and the question which assailed me for a long time was, 'Why me"? The more my husband, shekhar and I saw our little baby fighting for survival, more was the compassion that built within us, "If she can fight for herself, we thought we must accept and fight for her" Slowly, her innocence, little mischief and her way of doing things, her childish ways of talking grew upon us and became endearing".

The task in hand was quite a handful as children like Gauri, tend to be stubborn and once they decide it becomes very difficult to make them relent. They get stressed quickly, display signs of anger and tend to resist anything that they feel is a pressure for them. For the first 5 years, Sneha and Shekhar decided not to have another child, since Gauri needed full time attention and time.

Gauri was always under the care of Sneha and she devoted herself to her needs and upbringing. A differently abled child generally finds difficulty in co-ordination of body movement and synchronizing thought and action. Since, she had her inabilities, it was necessary to see to her educated in a compatible way and thus she was enrolled in National Open School to pursue her studies at home for class X. Alongside, she was given an exposure to tabla and harmonium in order to develop rhythmic alignment of mind and hand. On her doctor's suggestion, in order to help in improvement of motor skills, she was taken to the swimming coach Mr. Hrishikesh Tatooskar. A third year Engineering student, he was a man of immense drive, determination and passion. He observed Gauri for four days and asked Sneha to enroll Gauri in his class for basic swimming lessons. Hrishikesh was very particular and was determined to coach Gauri. A decision which became a major turning point in her life.

Gauri took to water like a fish and very soon showed remarkable improvement. She was quick to learn various styles and demonstrated grit and determination to rigorous training set for her by her coach Saurabh Deshpande. Grateful Sneha acknowledges, "Today Gauri has a huge success story, the credit must go to the passionate involvement and commitment of her coaches Hrushikesh, Saurabh, Harshad and Jitendra. They gave her an objective in life and proved to her that goals can be achieved if one has faith in oneself and determination to be passionate to fulfill the dreams".

Today, Gauri stands proud and is brimming with confidence because her achievements in swimming are commendable. She won Gold Medal in National Swimming Championships, Stood First at the National Level at Swimming Association of India Championships, Acted as a lead (her own character) in the National Award Winning Marathi motion picture "Yellow". She is undisputed in Maharashtra and entered River and Sea swimming successfully and has been successful in completing

6 km and 19km at a stretch. Such achievements are daunting and challenging for the capabilities of a normal child leave alone a specially abled one.

Another person who played a key role in elevating the self esteem and confidence of Gauri is her Bharatnatyam teacher Kalyani Kale. A clinical psychologist by profession, she took up this challenge and this enabled Gauri to perform on stage at many places including the famed Balgandharva Auditorium in Pune. She is completely free of stage fear and has the confidence to face audience of any size.

Gauri is no longer a student of National Open School. She was invited to join the regular Junior College by the Principal of SP College, Pune. Sneha had her reservations again "I was worried as to how Gauri can deal with the regular students and whether she can cope up with studies at such pace. I was surprisingly pleased to see that she could adapt herself well and was treated with affection by her class mates". Gauri adds, "Experience in my college is very pleasant. I have made many friends and nobody makes me feel I am different. I even go to movies with my friends". Gauri is a B. A. final year student and took up this challenge with ease. This was made possible with Shekar's support which was instrumental in enabling Gauri to tackle her studies with ease.

Gauri is very particular and maintains a very rigorous training schedule. Her schedule of daily practice includes exercise for 2-3 hours that includes 2-3 km running and swimming for 3 hours. She spends, at least, an hour for her studies, finds time for Bharatnatyam practice and weekly full body massage. Gauri says "I have made up my mind and now it is strongly embedded in me that I have to do it and I can; I believe that there is nothing one cannot achieve".

Thoughts In Retrospect

The emotional support and unstinted love and acceptance by her immediate family has played a singularly significant role in shaping

Gauri. The fact that Sneha could begin to empathize early with her motherly instincts overcoming the initial sense of despondency made a major change in approach towards her upbringing. Sneha deliberately delayed her second child as she felt it was necessary to give all her attention in the formative years without any diversion to Gauri. Thus, when Pallavi came along, mother, father and Gauri were ready to accept the new member into their fold. Pallavi was brought up in such a way that she very well understood the needs and limitations of her elder sister and became a big pillar of support. Sneha's eyes glint with pride "Pallavi is our blessing. She and Gauri are best friend's not mere sisters. Pallavi has been instrumental in enhancing the self confidence of Gauri in many ways. At swimming too, it was Pallavi who showed her how to dive as Gauri was initially fearful of diving. Pallavi would write speeches for Gauri and made her rehearse and very soon Gauri developed confidence and today she speaks on her own. She has been a major support system".

The biggest reason for her success in managing what many would perceive as a crisis of a lifetime is her ability to accept limitations and see strengths within the limitations. There are no perfect humans and what see as physical perfections have a large number of behavioral imperfections. Just because a child has limitations being specially abled that does not mean he/she has no strengths or areas of talent. "Had I adopted a fatalistic attitude accepting what has happened is destiny and approached it with despondency, Gauri would have been one among many; just an ordinary girl not an extraordinary one, as she is today". One person who remained in the background without whom there would be no story of Gauri, acknowledges Sneha "is my brother who was a source of infinite emotional strength for me throughout the initial years and later on to Gauri".

Bringing up a special child does not need special abilities but all it needs is accepting that such children are children too. When everyone rallies around and show support not sympathy, it acts as a catalyst for motivation. Those who happen to be parents of specially abled children must first get out of the syndrome of self pity. See their children as no different and make adjustments in life to meet the situation. One should look for support not sympathy because support gives solutions and alternatives and sympathy ends optimism. The focus should be on nurturing such children carefully in the first five to six years to give them confidence and involve them in such activities which match their abilities. Every child may not be Gauri but every child is as precious a child as Gauri. Sneha believes that **"Accept first, Act next and sustain throughout"** is the way out for those in similar situations.

Looking Glass: Outlook Ahead

Gauri having achieved substantial success; a lot more is expected; It's very important to reign in expectations. Sneha feels that whether a child is normal or specially abled, the trauma in a child's mind sets in because of expectations and failure to acknowledge performance. The other major aspect that hinders a child's growth is parental fear of failure. "Even I was always fearful that Gauri could never be an ace swimmer and that it would be a big psychological setback for her; I feared that she could never be on stage and I feared when she started sea swimming. Every time a new challenge would come up I would hesitate. I think we must learn to let children evolve to learn rather than evolve to succeed. Such an approach would surely put this fear of failure to rest".

A lot remains undone; for Sneha, it is still an ongoing commitment unwavering and infinite. For Gauri, it's all about being as normal as possible and showing that there are but no limits to what one can do. They both represent a symbiotic relationship which is ensconced in love, a deep sense of understanding, mutual respect and unending sense of being together as a "Binding Bond" forever.

■ ■ ■

Key Learning Values

Creating Self Confidence: Self confidence forms the basis of every action. In children this is an attribute that one needs to focus to enable a child to evolve.

Self Awareness: It is normal to be aware of one's strength's but self awareness would mean knowing the weakness and finding an alternate means to overcome the same.

Accepting Things One Cannot Change: It is very important in life to realize things that cannot change. The fact that Gauri is specially abled cannot change, so what can change is the approach to deal with the problem.

Avoid High Expectations and Setting Achievable Goals: In today's competitive environment, it is crucial to set achievable goals leading to a larger goal rather than focus on the unachievable.

Fear of Failure: Prevention is the first demonstration of fear of failure. It is important to give freedom to participate, freedom to win and freedom to lose. Everything must be part of the game.

Superimposing Beliefs: Elders/Parents invariably superimpose their reservations, fears and doubts on their children's capacity/capability. Children can do better than we expect and they must be allowed to flourish without hindrance.

Pandit Suresh Talwalkar

To evolve, a student of music must demonstrate six attributes.
Surrender- to guru and art form;
Devotion- to the cause;
Hardship- to demonstrate ability to with stand;
Sincerity- to show commitment;
Loyalty- to words the art form and the guru;
Punctuality- to demonstrate consistency and regularity.

CREATING
A RHYTHM OF LIFE

Pandit Suresh Talwalkar

The Magic of Music

Music has a magic because it has an effect of transformation. Sometimes it transforms emotions and at times it transforms the practitioners. Such an effect is most common but there are very few who contribute in transforming the approach to music itself and one such unique maestro of music is Suresh. Not because he is an expert exponent of Tabla, but because he was instrumental in giving a new, distinct and an individual identity to Tabla transforming it from a supportive role to main stream role. He was one person who brought the magic of tabla from the silhouette to project it to a place it deserves by positioning it in the hearts of music lovers.

Music & folklore

As part of folklore, it is said that when Lord Krishna played his basuri (Flute) at Brindavan, all the birds and animals in the forest would get mesmerized by the melodious sound and gather around him as if in a trance. Ustad Abdul Karim Khan, a vocal exponent of Kirana Gharana, was no less. A name to reckon with, he was known to be a singer par excellence and was acknowledged as the "Guru of Guru's".

The story dates back to pre independent India. One day, as he was practicising as part of his daily "Riyaz" (committed musical practice) at his residence in Meerut, a very well dressed gentleman, fully attired in a suit with a bowler hat and a cane in tow, with a pompous demeanor, entered his house. The Ustad's house was quite Spartan and most of the belongings were simple and associated to music. He was singing, sitting on the floor, which was the usual practice, with some disciples in attendance. Seeing the gentleman, he stopped his 'Riyaz' and greeted him, speculating why such a person should come to his humble home. After making him comfortable on the only sofa in the room and some refreshment, he enquired about the purpose of the visit. To his surprise, the gentleman replied that he came because he wanted to learn music. Ustad Abdul Karim Khan was abit exasperated by his demeanor but did not let that show on his face. He thought to himself "to learn music one would have to first demonstrate submission of oneself and absence of ego, let me put him to test". He looked at him and in a crisp yet polite tone asked him to come at the same time, after a week. Next week, at the designated time, the scene was identical; Ustad on ground sitting for his 'Riyaz' as the gentleman came in; The Ustad made no effort to acknowledge him and continued. The gentleman made himself comfortable on the sofa. Ustad wanted the gentleman to realize that he needs to sit in front of him on ground and he did not wish to tell him. He said to himself "Let this be a test of my music, whether it can make him realize and come down on his own". He stared singing a 'raag' (form of Hindustani music having melodic shape, rhythm and ornamentation) in a melodious low pitch. In order to hear it better, the gentleman shifted forward; seeing that the Ustad lowered his pitch further causing the gentleman to bend his head and further inch closer to the sofa's edge. Observing his keenness, Ustad, further lowered the pitch and the gentleman got up and sat down in front of the Ustad on the ground. The Ustad smiled as he stopped his singing and told him "For today, this much is enough, we will start your training from next week".

Eyes wide open; a curious Suresh was animatedly listening to this story from his Guru Nivruti Bauva. It left an imprint on three counts, firstly, it made him realize that learning music is not technique through lessons but needs submission of self, secondly, the subtle manner in which the Ustad used music to test the intent of the prospect to make him realize rather than explain, and thirdly, how the Ustad accepted him as his disciple with open arms on observing the change. Subtle restraint, positive intent, learning through observation were the significant lessons which stayed as value additions to his character. Such Guru-Shishya (teacher-disciple) interaction was to be the foundation of a tradition called "Parampara" (a tradition of long standing practice for continuity) which was an essential part of learning music from masters by staying, being, watching and imbibing by living with gurus.

A Flashback

Dattatreya Mahadev Talwalkar was a passionate musician. Though he never had formal training, he played Pakhawaj, Harmonium and Tanpura well. For him accompanying, his uncle, Ramakrishna Dhole, a singer of folklore belonging to Kirtana (divotional singing usually accompanied by an instrument) Parampara and an exponent of "Naradeeyaa Sangeet" (form of semi classical folk music) was a unique experience. He performed along with him in these recitals which attracted huge crowds those days even necessitating use of police at times for crowd control. Dattatreya Mahadev Talwarkar, aware that he lacked formal training in classical music, nursed a dream that his son Suresh would follow his footsteps and excel by going through a formal learning process. Music was very much part of the household and it was no surprise when Suresh took to it most spontaneously.

From a very young age of three, he began learning and by the time he was eight, he was sent to his first Guru, Pandit Vinayak Rao. Thus began his delightful and delectable journey into the world of music. Many years down the line, Suresh emerged as a maestro of repute. He decided that his contributions to music cannot just rest on his personal laurels but a more proactive role needs to be played by propagating music in the true spirit of "Parampara". With this quest in mind, he worked to establish a music school unique in concept and exceptional in execution.

Usual Yet Unusual

Usual, because it's a school housed in a bungalow. It's unusual because it's a school but does not look and feel like one; students are few who sport a dreamy look as they seem to be in search of personal quest; the master is one; not just a physical entity but someone larger than life and the knowledge they seek is not taught but acquired and learning is passionate. Throughout the day and even beyond, the environs are resonant with the sounds of Tabla and other instruments which the students are hoping to master. Suresh Talwalkar, the tabla maestro presides over this school with childlike enthusiasm and day after day providing an avenue to these learners through guidance, interaction, practice and personal example to understand the essence of music and in the process mirroring them to part be of a legacy that seems a throw back into history.

A Gurukul! In the twentieth century, midst of a bustling metropolis; sounds more fictional than real.It may not look like what one reads in epics, but it is simple, Spartan and symbolic. It propagates living, working, learning and feeling the musical ambience at all times. It positions the relationship between the Guru and the Shishsya at a different level making it more binding and influential. Suresh feels that the ability of a guru to propagate his talent depends greatly on his students. How they respond to situations to facilitate the aspirations of their Guru is very significant. Suresh neither had the capacity nor the space to follow his dream of spreading music through a Gurukul model. The solution came from his disciples, Dr. Srinivas Rao and Mukta Rao. Srinivas, a medical doctor and a tabla player and Mukta, a classical dancer. Prior to their immigration to United Kingdom, they offered their bungalow to their Guru to be used by him for as long as he needs for establishing a Gurukul. In that bungalow, the Gurukul stands today offering training to over 50 students; not as a commercial venture but as a contribution with a missionary zeal. Suresh does not charge any fees for teaching. The students pay a very nominal amount toward administrative costs. The group consists of students from all over India, from Rajasthan to Chennai and Delhi to Assam. The cosmopolitan nature lends a national character to his Gurukul.

Under the Banyan Tree

Suresh was fortunate to thrive under a banyan tree. The art form symbolizing the tree and evolution of multiple skills under various gurus, representing the growth under the protective shadow of the tree. Suresh attributes his success entirely to the learning's he gained by living with his Gurus. Music unlike formal education needs greater interaction and higher influence. While formal education is direct and technical, learning an art form is perceptual and felt. How is a Gurukul experience different? He explains "Music can be best learnt only if there is a co-existence of an intimate personal relationship between the teacher and the taught". Four things become significant;

"Shastra, Tantra, Vidya and Kala". Shastra (Vocabulary of Music) implies 'science' of music which needs to be understood; Tantra (Technique) meaning the technical sequence of learning which has to be taught; Vidya (Knowledge) denotes 'matter' which has to be given and Kala(art) is symbolic of Sanskar (culture) without which the form does not transform to the level of art.

Sanskar is an outcome of two important attributes i.e., Sahawas and Shravan. Shahawas meaning co-existing at all times with the Guru and Shravan emphasizing listening to the guru. The true beauty of learning is distinguished from formal learning by understanding that "music is not about matter but all about manner". The Gurukul concept would entail therefore complete submission of the student towards the art form and his Guru and complete acceptance of the Guru as a commitment. There is nothing except a mutual pledge to empower each other.

Having started early, Suresh was focused only on Tabla and did not acquire formal educational qualifications. In spite of lacking in formal degrees, still he stands acknowledged as a respected teacher known for intellectual and artistic excellence. He authored a book titled "Avartan" which has become a reference book to those who wish to learn about the intricacies of teaching and learning processes of music as an art form.

Explaining further, Suresh says "From my four Gurus, I have acquired four distinct attributes which enabled me to remain rooted to ground realities. It is this sanskar, that enabled me to rise above the race for recognition and made me a disciple of "Kala" (Artistic rendition of music)".

Talking about Pandit Pandarinath, he recollects "I have never seen him grow old, he was picture of perfect fitness even in his old age, always erect, always at 'riyaz' always learning and always motivated to teach. He is to me an ultimate example of motivation". Recounting his experience with Pandit Vinayak Rao, Suresh recollects, "He was a picture of humility. One could never ever find in him even an iota of pride and he taught me the importance of humility which has enabled me to retain my mental balance in the face of success, praise and criticism". Talking about Pandit Ramnad Ishwaran, Suresh acknowledges "I owe to this guru, the knowledge of understanding the intricacies of 'laya' and 'taal' which became the foundation for my success as an artist who could integrate Carnatic rythm with Hindustani taal". Pandit Gajanan Rao Joshi paved the way for understanding the distinction between "Kala (Art)" and "Kalakar (Artist)". "I can vividly recall his words, Kala is far superior than the kalakar. However big an artist to be, remember that the knowledge one possesses is like a drop in the ocean. If Kala is a mountain, the Kalakar will always be at the bottom and whatever he does, he just touches the base".

Down to Mother Earth

It was a very satisfying trip abroad. Suresh had returned after performing in many countries and having received a lot of praise, was the centre of adulation. He began to consider himself to have perfected the art form. In his eagerness to impress Pandit Vinayak Rao, he boasted about his exploits. At that time, his Guru was mentoring disciples of Suresh, some of whom were already well known. Suresh recounts "As I began talking big, my Guruji started playing a very basic "Theka". (Theka being a set of syllables used to denote a particular "Tal" (System of rhythm). For example "Dha Dhin Dhin Dha" could be manifested in multiple forms which depended on the expertise of the practitioner. That day, I was totally aghast and surprised to see him play this and soon realized the beauty of it and the difference in it. Soon my gaze at him turned to amazement as I could realize that it was in a totally different form, unknown to me".

"Guruji could gauge and read three things from my eyes. Firstly, he read, I was initially wondering why something seemingly simple was being practiced, secondly, he could make out that I realized how beautifully it was played and thirdly that, he guessed that I did not know how to play it so well". Suresh could not resist asking him to teach him this new variation. With a wry smile Guruji said "Aap Itne bade kalaakar ho, main aap ko kaise sikha sakta hoon" (You are such an established artist, how is it possible for me to teach you now). The message went straight home and I understood that even at the basic level, there are manifestations of art that are yet to be learnt and thus I never boasted again".

Matter Vs Manner

In the world of music, while matter can be learnt by any source or teacher, the manner can only be learnt by observing gurus. Who is a Guru? A person, an expert, a qualified specialist or a consummate artist? Suresh explains, "A Guru is what I call a "Tatwa". He is an embodiment of Principles and Essence of true values of life". He symbolizes all aspects of reality of music in all conceivable forms. It's because of this that they can inspire action in their disciples and create a desire to excel through "Riyaz". 'Riyaz' is the foundation for understanding the "Manner" in music. In explicit terms, one may conclude 'Riyaz' as practice and continuous 'Riyaz' thus should lead to excellence but that never happens. 'Riyaz' can lead to excellence only if it combines four important concepts; Sharir (Body), Man (Mind), Buddhi (Intelligence) and Aatma (Soul). Once these attributes combine, it elevates 'Riyaz' from mere 'Abhayas' (Practice) to 'Sadhana'. Once in this state, an artist gets the first emotional connect relating with 'Anubhav' (Experience) leading to 'Anubhuti' (Ecstasy). A 'Guru' is thus an instrument who enables his students to elevate to the level of Sadhana. One most important lesson a guru can bestow on his mentees is facilitation of self realization from time to time. This would entail showing the disciples where they have to go and letting them know where they are; this is what Suresh experienced on that day, when his Guru Pandit Vinayak Rao, indirectly pointed out that he can no longer be taught, there by indicating to Suresh, that he is not as accomplished as he is thinking himself to be.

Thus the emotive components of learning like Riyaz, Sadhana, Anubhav and Anubhuti can happen only when transformation of learning music changes from matter to manner.

Suresh accepts that the total Gurukul concept may not be the call of the day. He also understands the fact that formal education is the need of the hour to be able to handle the challenges of life. He therefore encourages his students to pursue formal education alongside structured training in music.

Speaking about his success, he believes that when one is fully committed and places faith, hard work and diligence, there will be a protective hand of fate that will intervene to ensure that one's needs are looked after. He quotes his own example that despite not having any formal qualification, he is acknowledged not only as an artist and teacher but also for his intellectual insights.

Classical Music: A Look Ahead

Music is a way of life and it has defined and defied changes enveloping the society from centuries. In evolution, change is constant and anything that does not adapt faces extinction and music is no exception. The influx of technology and influence of western music have significantly made an imprint on the current generation. Notwithstanding these, "Classical music", says Suresh, "has the resilience not only to withstand but to also redefine itself. The challenge I feel is not influx of external musical influences, it is the changing attitudes of the society towards music. The shift from art form to gain form. Younger generation is impatient for success, gain and recognition and hence the focus of learning has re-aligned from delight and contentment to entertainment and gratification".

In today's context, for students of music however few attributes remain unchanged. Suresh reinforces, "A budding artist has to demonstrate these attributes to be a musician of value namely; Surrender implying completely giving up oneself to the Guru and music; Devotion meaning undying commitment to the cause; Hardship denoting willingness and ability to withstand sustained difficulty; Sincerity signifying total involvement and commitment, Loyalty symbolizing the spirit to protect and defend the cause of Kala (Art) and support the Kalakar (Artist) and lastly Punctuality having connotation of regularity in 'Riyaz' and adherence to schedules.

Suresh feels blessed because of the Grace of God's benign hand in all his endeavours. His family is an example of commitment to music. His wife Padma Talwalkar, is an acknowledged vocalist, his son Satyajit and daughter Shravani are both accomplished players of tabla and are recipients of Sangeet Natak Academy Bismillah Khan Yuva Puraskar.

Suresh has an unending list of accolades and rewards. While he acknowledges each with utmost humility, the one's that gave him a sense of deep satisfaction are Padma Shree by the President of India and the title of "Taal Yogi" bestowed on him by Jagadguru Shri Shankaracharya. He carries all this with grace with no pretension or pride.

Its evening and as he walks out of his school gate; not into sunset but to brighter sunrise beyond, a strong over powering sense of hope, optimism and confidence is perceptible. *"The Magic of Music"* he says *will prevail to strengthen and sustain classical music enabling it to reign supreme.*

■ ■ ■

Key Learning Values

Passion and Devotion: Be it music or any form of activity these two attributes will define the approach and outcome.

Humility: It is important to realize the difference between learning and the learned. A learned man is always learning and hence humble; therefore this realization is very essential as one grows in any profession.

Unending Learning: Success in any profession is an outcome of unending learning. The focus should never shift.

Commitment to Mission: Once undertaken, the objective should always be to pursue with best efforts. The intent must be clearly defined.

Patience to Evolve: There are no shortcuts and one must develop a long time perspective of success and develop patience to evolve.

Focus on Excellence not Recognition: It is important to have a focus on ensuring excellence in performance every time. Recognition is a natural outcome of excellence and not vice versa.

Abhijit Pawar

"Change is never systemic. In a true sense, it cannot be enforced. For change to occur it must be believed and accepted. Action for change must be focused not at the mind but at the mind set".

REFLECTIONS OF AN INTREPID OPTIMIST

Abhijit Pawar

Spirited School Days

Best reflective moments of life are usually centered around school days. Head pointed at the Sun and feet on the move, a fearless carefree attitude and an open mind add to the beauty of life and make growing up a journey of joy. Affluence, position, caste or color rarely figure in the scheme of things and biases that cloud the grown up minds elude the growing ones making friendships and building relationships easy and strong. School becomes a crucible of values; one learns not just by learning what is taught but by experiencing the pleasure of growing up with caring and sense of sharing, observing and supporting one another where ever and when ever.

For Abhijit, studying at Loyala High School was a pure joy. Good in studies, active in games, participative in numerous activities, with a fine circle of friends, a bit of mischief and a lot of spirit, Loyola High school was just the place one wished to be. Teachers were endearing and exceptional; they were examples of behavior and guided students to focus towards good conduct not by force but reinforcing through personal example of exemplary conduct. Growing up those days recalls Abhijit "Was a lot of fun. We grew up together, playing, fighting, studying and sharing; always as a part of a group and never alone. We learnt that learning to live as a part of community is more important than growing up just an individual".

Unlike many boys of his age, Abhijit was focused. He believed that whatever he decided to do must be done to best of his ability. It was not in him to be a jack of all and be the master of none. He also remembers that even as early as his school days, there was an inner desire to make a contribution by doing something significant. This positive approach made him excel in school not just in academics but also in various activities. The fruits of his consistence were recognized when he was selected for the top school award "The Best Student in class X". This was a dream come true for Abhijit as this strengthened his resolve and self-esteem since the award was purely on merit and getting it proved to him that he had it in him to excel.

Values Beneth the Shield of Simplicity

Abhijit's family was quite influential. His father was actively associated with the leading newspaper "Sakal" and was also in business. They were well networked in the city and had reckonable connections with the "who is who" in political and social circles. The family was fairly affluent. It was very easy for his parents to let children grow in an affluence and remain connected with an environment which would have made them more conscious of their status. This possibly would have denied them the awareness to be humble and open. Being a man of values and strong beliefs, Pratap Rao Pawar deliberately chose to let his children be unaware of this family legacy. Abhijit grew up in a small 500 Sq ft flat, he always observed his mother taking a two wheeler "Luna" to the market and buy vegetables and manage home frugally. He went to school on a bicycle and he swears that only in college, he became aware that his father was fairy wealthy and very influential in the city of Pune. Even at college, when many of his friends would travel on their own scooters, he always travelled in a bus. He recalls his father's response to his request for a scooter, "grow up first, earn next and buy thereafter". It was during his college days that he realized the disadvantages of being associated with a family of repute and influence. It hurt him initially when he heard people talk, that his award as best student at school and his appointment as captain of the State Junior Hockey team were because of influence, though these achievements were totally on merit. This made him understand that he needs to be more sensitized to such opinion and such reactions would be an occupational hazard, being from a prominent family. This made him realize that greater transparency is the only way to deal with such opinions and he must develop resilience to accept them in his stride. Learning to tackle one's own battles on one's own strengths, was something he realized quite early. Abhijit attributes his parental influence in growing up stages and the family environment rooted in simplicity as two important factors that kept him grounded to realities of life. Family is always the nodal point for developing the personality and character. What happens within and what is demonstrated is what matters in the end. Two significant incidents in the growing stages of Abhijit have played a defining role in influencing his belief in values and ethics.

After his schooling, Abhijit joined Fergusson College for his intermediate. He was good in studies and took an active part in sports and took to playing hockey passionately. His preoccupation with sport and extracurricular activities resulted in low attendance. Those days students having low attendance were not permitted to appear in the final examination. It was expected that the student's parents meet the Principal and tender an apology for the lapse. Many of Abhijit's friends were in this category and their parents did the needful enabling them to be cleared for appearing in the exam. From Abhijit's point of view, he expected his father to do the same. When Abhijit approached his father, he asked him who was responsible for the absence. Abhijit told him that it was actually his fault that he missed college. "You must learn to take responsibility for your actions. If the rule says that below 75% are to be debarred from appearing in the examination then so be it. I will not apologize for you because it will amount my taking the responsibility for your fault and if I do so, throughout your life you will look for other's shoulders whenever you falter". It was simply unbelievable and shocking for Abhijit; he was a good student, and not meeting the Principal would result in a loss of one full year and all other students in a similar state were appearing for the exam. "I felt demolished and was livid with annoyance and could not understand why he did this to me. I felt he was being an egotist and unconcerned. I did lose a year. The incident and his words remained within and I realized when I grew up that I gained much more because this made me understand the significance of an action, respect for the rules and meaning of being accountable to one's actions".

The second important incident related to his request for Rs 50 for his driving license. It was a common practice and knowledge, those days that for a bribe of Rs 50 to the RTO inspector, one would get the driving license without appearing in the mandatory driving test. "When I told this to my father, he looked at me with an icy stare and said You try that and I will ensure you go to jail". Abhijit went back to the RTO and followed the correct procedure, stood in line, paid the requisite fees and secured his license the right way after passing the test. "It taught me not to accept short cuts and encourage wrong because we wish to make our lives easy. This also made me understand that the difficulties people who cannot afford to bribe undergo and gave me the sense of empathy to understand problems at grass root level".

Choice of Being Different

The choices of career were indeed limited. It was the "Devil's Alternative" for most students and Abhijit was no exception. Some kind of herd mentality prevailed which compelled good students to gravitate towards Engineering or Medicine. Abhijit chose Engineering and he secured admission in Mechanical Engineering stream, in Walchand College of Engineering, Sangli. It was more like a bandwagon syndrome that made Abhijit choose this option. Most of his friends chose engineering and his father too wanted him to be one.

With very little or no pocket money to support his expenses, Abhijit started his first entrepreneurial venture in a small scale in his second year. He started share broking and began to make enough money to support his needs at the college. Soon after acquiring his engineering degree, for some time he focused his attention on financial sub broking. His father was well established and Abhijit could have joined in any of his ventures or could have easily found himself a job through family influence. He resisted the very idea of employment and showed keenness to pursue his own dream through entrepreneurship. He was all set to experience the feel of devising something new. Unafraid of hardships, he was well prepared to deal with new challenges and difficulties. Borrowing Rs 10, 000 from his father, he embarked on a venture which had everything at stake; his money, reputation, family and personal credibility.

From sub broking, he joined his friends to open a software company and working with focus, very soon they found business growing in their favor. Ups and downs, profits and gains along with losses and lows became an integral part. For over a decade, the company grew substantially establishing business in India and abroad. Abhijit moved abroad for a few years and with the business in a good nick, it was more or less certain that he would continue to be away.

He recalls "I started as complete novice. No advice, no guidance and no experience. All I had was a fierce determination, self confidence and a will to succeed. Jumping into the unknown had its own advantages, may be ignorance was a bliss which made me fearless. It was the challenge that attracted and inspired me".

Abhijit acknowledges his father's tacit support. When he announced his intention to start on his own his father encouraged. "He never once tried to dissuade me. He knew that I had made up my mind and would not relent. He made it easy for me by his tacit mentoring, encouragement and confidence which spurred me work harder to succeed". These years added maturity to Abhijit and made him competent to handle situations and capable of being a successful entrepreneur.

Return of the Prodigal

With success came money and Abhijit began to introspect. The call within him was still unaddressed. There was a voice inside reminding him of the void of an unfinished agenda. The uneasy feeling of having left the motherland began to exert more and more. It was around this time, his father expressed his desire to have Abhijit back to take over the reins of Sakal and other businesses. To Abhijit, it seemed like an opportunity in waiting; his calling was there to see and he packed his bags to return back to India.

Understanding the business of Sakal was a new learning experience. Sakal was a very well established newspaper enjoying extensive goodwill and trust within the environment. In the initial stages, it appeared to Abhijit, the way the paper was managed was more patriarchal and benevolent rather than business like. He looked at the paper from a business perspective and his father looked at it as an institution with an entity. As he began to work, the cause of the newspaper and its ethos began to grow on him and very soon he found his calling. He took to media eagerly and understood that for Sakal what mattered was "Return on Respect not Return on Investment". It was ingrained in every one that Sakal was a paper "which was trusted by the people; it was made for the people and it belonged to the people". The ethos of Sakal represented contributory journalism which played an active binding role in the society. The focus of the business approach was first on service and next on profit and not vice versa.

Abhijit explains "The role of Sakal is that of Narada Muni in our scriptures. Narada was known to question people in such a way that it would extract right actions. It was his question to Vali the Dacoit which transformed him into Valmiki, the erudite Sage who wrote the Ramayana. Thus Sakal assumes the role of asking questions which are intended to transform lives and governance. Like Narada, who was known to be good at networking with all the three worlds, Sakal too is expected to network with everyone to get the right thing going". Sakal then was more then just a newspaper, it was a reflection of living and reflected a way of life. Service and socially relevant activities became an intrinsic part and parcel of Sakal. For Abhijit, this was the call of his heart he was awaiting.

A Mission Called Sakal

Being at the helm of a media house like Sakal enabled a ringside view of the issues that ail the society at large. It is up to the media to either sensationalize these issues and make a gain out of it or take up the issues to sensitize the society to enable gain to the society. To Abhijit, who imbibed the essence of values and culture through his father, family and the ethos of Sakal, the option never existed. He began to commit himself and his team with reinforced vigor to use Sakal as an instrument of change. Deciding an attempting to create a change in the society and embarking on a mission to enforce was a daunting challenge. In a country as diverse and as divided as ours, attempts by themselves become a task to be reckoned with. Abhijit's perspective is rather unique "I believe change is not systemic. One cannot structure a change, it cannot be enforced; it has to be believed to be accepted. Actions for change must be focused not at the mind but at the mindset. We have to begin, persevere and sustain. I tell my team its a thousand year battle, what has begun to day cannot be expected to show results tomorrow. I have taken a real long term view and that's what drives us". The journey must begin and the one must enjoy the process by connecting as many people to the problem as possible. Social change can neither be evaluated like an individual performance nor can be quantifiable by the number of projects or actions undertaken. The impact of actions for change can only be visible across a spectrum of time and this is a function of commitment and that seems to be in abundance in Abhijit and his team. How does one remain enthused and motivated and never be bogged down by the challenges and hurdles? The answer lies in his inner strength and the major source of this strength is his Guruji, Dr. Balaji Tambe, who introduced him to the world of spirituality through a unique medium of Ayurveda. Abhijit feels that spiritualism is understanding ways of life and meaning of existence and is unrelated to religion. Every individual in times of stress needs a guiding light and this light in the form of a mentor can channelize energy in the right direction. Abhijit reinforces this with great emphasis and believes that his Guru was instrumental in shaping spiritual thinking and understanding which reinforced his character and elevated his thinking.

It is this holistic perception which, he says, is paving way for the contributory role of Sakal Group. Understanding the huge need and the gap the requirements, few areas of priority have been identified. While everything may be important, everything cannot be given importance and this is the foundation of understanding the reason for priority. The areas which he is keen to address are Drought and Water Management, Vegetable Farming and Individual well being through diet awareness and lastly focus on Infrastructure development. In short, the gamut of these areas of choice is very extensive; it is his endeavor to create greater awareness among people with respect to utilization of water through channelizing river water to better use; create a no drought scenario by ensuring adequacy of supply by promoting remunerative farming to financially empower farming as a profession and address aspects of infrastructure which in the long run provide stability and access to the community at large.

Reminiscences and Reflections

Does he think he has achieved success? Abhijit feels it is not really the measure that matters; what truly matters is how much is done; how much more can be done and how well one is poised to do? He reflects upon himself and concedes that in the given span a lot has been achieved and lot more remains in the pipe line. Is it an easy task to balance the needs of business, requirements of the society and demands of personal and family life? To him everything is possible if one has the mind set. He attributes few things that enable him to balance the challenging needs which seek attention in equal measure. "Being a learner always helps in being grounded, understanding the importance of priority ensures time is slotted for the one that needs attention, ability to be on the correct path provides strength to face adversities, a questioning attitude to see and learn to match fast changing environment, helps me to keep pace with the changes". He feels the generation of today has tremendous access and technology has become a part and parcel of our daily lives. It is not what is changing every day but how quickly one can adapt to these, to make them part of our system that matters in future. Curiosity, inquisitiveness and intensity are the cardinal characteristics one must develop to be in the race for survival.

When one is young, vibrant and positive, with resources and capabilities; embellished with a strong desire to make way for a better tomorrow, the future seems bright. Abhijit looks ahead like he did in his school days with his head up pointed to the Sun and feet on the move, with an attitude of carefree positivity. With time on his side, his dreams find a "Reflection in his thoughts as an Intrepid Optimist" to inspire those around him "To do good; To do more and To do it well".

■ ■ ■

Key Learning Values

Rooted to Reality: Understanding the ground realities and developing a realistic and humble approach enables development of better personality.

Values System and Integrity: Family values are very important and play a significant role on the minds of children. It is essential to realize that a child learns from observation not oral communication. Being is more important than saying.

Persistence and Patience: Success is an outcome of these two characteristics. There are and there will never be shortcuts.

Identifying the Call Within: Every thing we do may not always be what we want to do. One must try to see how best one can find a way to do at we do.

Being A Student Always: Learning never ever ceases. It is a misnomer to relate learning to education and degrees. The process must continue lifelong.

Learning to Prioritize: Life is always offering multiple alternatives which compete for time. While everything we seek seem important, everything cannot be important. Identifying what is needed and what needs time is an art that must be cultivated.

Sudhir Gadgil

Willingness to commit, willingness to persevere, willingness to demonstrate integrity with honest intentions will always create a credible personality so essential to be in public life.

A PASSIONATE INTERLOCUTOR

Sudhir Gadgil

Ingraining Good from the Great

The year was 1978. Sudhir was anxious yet confident; overpowering sense of excitement was mounting from within. He was waiting to interview right outside the Office of the Prime Minister of India. To be among those to be given such an opportunity by itself was an achievement. Sudhir was young and well equipped to face the challenge that awaited him. He was ushered inside to be face to face with one of the most dynamic ladies of India, Mrs. Indira Gandhi. Graceful, elegant and dignified, her demeanor was compelling and strong and her smile warm and welcoming with an overwhelming aura. Sudhir, in spite of his political affiliation at cross roads with the Congress, was unequivocally impressed. He acknowledged her as a legend.

People who adorn greatness are no different from others. They do everything the way everyone else does. What characterizes their greatness is the way they do it and the manner in which they execute it. The great become great because they tacitly and implicitly create a lifetime impact by their words, deeds, behavior and actions. Mrs. Gandhi was one such person. Having done many interviews, Sudhir was able to execute his task with expected ease and comfort. As the interaction was about to conclude Mrs. Gandhi said something which became a lifetime dictum for Sudhir to follow.

She said "I was six years of age, when my father, Pandit Jawaharlal Nehru, told me that every day before going to bed two things must be done. Writing one page in a diary describing the day and reading few pages from a book without fail. I do it every day even now and that relieves my stress for the day. You must try it too". Sudhir was so influenced by this suggestion that, he began to follow this meticulously. This habit transform him as a person quite unaware as to how the change came about. Writing a page a day, enabled an honest introspection of the day and created forethought for the next. Regular reading tremendously improved my personality and made me wiser, knowledgeable and objective.

Learning the "Art of Dialogue"

When seen in retrospect, childhood seems a distant dream. Dream more so because of the harmonious upbringing creating a valuable living experience through building and sustaining relationships. The joint family environment created with spontaneity lessons which enabled Sudhir to learn how to listen, convince, deliberate, enforce or comply. Sometimes you gave in and sometimes others would. Everything was meant to be shared and sharing was the expectation. It was a "We Culture" that prevailed and not an "I Culture". Recalls Sudhir "Being together, we learnt the need to accept the other person's positive and negative traits. This taught me how to overlook negative points and appreciate positive one's . It taught the importance of being accommodative and adaptive and convinced me that long term need of being together is more important than short term gain of being right".

This was the origin of the first most important lesson in communication; knowing the significance of "Dialogue". Solving differences by meaningful dialogue since childhood, imbibed the firm conviction that communication and deliberation through dialogue are the foundation for effective coexistence.

It is said that "A family which eats together, stays together". Throughout childhood, Sudhir was exposed to this adage. All family members would get together at dinner time, this was the time for exchange of views, information and appreciation and at times for mild reprimand in case anyone was found to be errant. Sudhir still emulates these values at home. His 90 year old mother and 94 year old father stay with him and so does his son's family.

Making of a Journalist

While the growing up phase at home was instrumental in setting the tone for balanced thinking and emotionally strong personality; his school and college days were significant in reinforcing the values learnt at home. Sudhir went to Nutan Marathi Vidyalaya, which was the pioneering school focusing on extracurricular activities along with academic rigor. Prof Narlikar, the Principal, was a role model. At the entrance of the school, there was a board showing the names of school toppers. All students entering had to pass by looking at it. Sudhir attributes his quest for excellence in his profession to the silent impression this board exerted throughout his school days. It was like someone always reminding "To be on the top, strive to work hard". The school also had a unique club called "Chamatkar Mandal" (Marvel Club) which taught magic tricks. The art of captivating the spectators by communication and drawing their attention was an important lesson learnt by him. Enacting these magic tricks made him realize the need for a continuous dialogue in order to mesmerize the audience. During the summer vacations, the school used to organize Bar soap selling competition. Students were expected to be salesmen and proceed house to house to sell bar soaps. For three successive years, Sudhir was adjudged the winner. This activity made him realize the art of convincing as an important ingredient of communication. The soap had to be sold to people unknown to him and the only medium was effectiveness of communication. Understanding the product, communication through dialogue, listening to others views, putting forth a viable point of view, deliberations and discussions, captivating by expression were some of the significant view points Sudhir developed during his school days.

A very interesting perspective of Sudhir emerged and became noticeable during his college days. It is here, he first got an opportunity to be on stage in front of a large audience for annual gatherings. He did mimicry of various hawkers by imitating their unique style of calling and selling. The good response to his performances gave him the confidence to face a large audience, which ultimately reflected in his success as an anchor in the years ahead. What is it that made people appreciate his performance? Sudhir was an expert in observing and understanding the behavior of people. His keen sense of observation would reveal new perspectives about people which he was able to capture and represent. He used every possible opportunity to be on stage either performing or anchoring programs at college which drew a lot of applause and support. Though idea of Journalism as a career came in late, he did realize that settling down to a mundane 9 to 5 job in a bank after B.Com was not his cup of tea. The potential lay elsewhere in public domain and he made up his mind to make a foray into it. It is during this period, Sudhir started a unique activity. He began to collect information regarding important people in Maharashtra and began to maintain separate files. What began as an activity assumed tidal proportions as he collected information in 3600 files on various persons. This work became the foundation for his preparation for interviews in future as he had plethora of inputs which he could use during interviews. Sudhir claims that preparing these files was tremendous experience and from these inputs he learnt a lot as each file represented the strengths, successes and weaknesses of eminent people. Attending speeches and maintaining notes as he listened was another activity that greatly helped Sudhir. It developed his keen listening skills and fine tuned his grasping power. This ensured, Sudhir understood the effectiveness of oratory and the different styles of speaking and language made him realize that his career is cut out for something in public domain and that would be journalism.

Initial part of his career was rough. He wore multiple hats and did a wide array of jobs in a day. He would travel from Pune to Mumbai and back for seven long years. Indeed those were physically challenging, mentally exhaustive and yet emotionally stimulating days. His day would begin with a routine many would find it difficult. "I would start at 5.30 am with translation, copywriting and the collection of the news material for the morning news at Akashwani at 7.15 am. Thereafter by the Madras express and go to Mumbai by 12.30 pm. I would do the voice over in many advertising agencies, followed by translation of advertisements from English to Marathi. After one hour voice over, two hours of copy writing translation, I would to go to the TV station for conducting the interviews. I also took up anchoring in a big way and began by anchoring for musical programs, usually in Worli, Dadar or Girgaum. As owning a home in Bombay was unaffordable, there was no option but to commute. It was usual to return to Pune by 1.30 am. This routine continued unhindered for over 7 years. In short, the tough regime made him do collection of information for news, news reading on radio, voice over, translations, copy writing, conduct interviews on TV and anchoring. Undeterred, he never looked back and put his heart and soul in whatever he did and did it well. This helped him to build a huge base in the media and the advertising agency field, which he could leverage effectively in later years.

Another significant trait, Sudhir imbibed from compiling files on his upbringing is the ability to tackle negativity. He reiterates that compiling files on each of the 3600 personalities has given him one lesson at least thus making him more complete, mature and understanding. Through these lessons, he acquired an ability to deal with aggressive responses of the interviewees and hostile situations very effectively without causing distress, anger or antagonism during his interviews. Not withstanding the differences of opinion, Sudhir always ensured that dignity and decorum of the interviewee was well maintained.

Impact and Influence

Sudhir was unique because he blended character, commitment, integrity and impartial conduct as significant attributes when dealing with people of eminence. This enabled him to create a name for himself paving way for many successes. He narrates "There was a time in 1974, when Balasaheb Thackeray, the Shiv Sena Patriarch, refused to give interviews even to well known anchors like Nikhil Wagle. My first request was accepted and I got this opportunity. I prepared very well and conducted his interview. This become the starting point of a very long personal association; I conducted 13 interviews and had the privilege of filming him on a non political theme". The bonding was so strong that Sudhir became the Editor of "Samana", the newspaper which is the mouthpiece of Shiv Sena. A task that was very challenging considering the political ideology of the organization.

Sudhir maintains that to be a successful interviewer, one needs to understand the person well. In addition to the factual knowledge, it is always important to know the likes and dislikes, so that these can be used to either make a headway or deflect controversies. Making the interviewee comfortable and bringing them to ease by creating a feeling of goodwill and trust was his strong point. "One of the most challenging tasks was to interview and film Shantanu Rao Kirloskar, noted industrialist in Maharashtra. It was difficult because, he was resisting to be interviewed and his children wanted a film to be made on him. I studied a lot to know about him and understood that he liked to discuss about Operas which were his passion. Meeting him in his attractive garden, I addressed him as "Balwant" like all others and began my discussion asking him to show me his vast collection of operas especially the Sydney Opera. Excited to share, he became involved in an animated discussion, which I navigated to my interview requirements. On conclusion of the interview, as I was about to leave, he looked at me with a twinkle in his eye and said" Sudhir, I knew what you were up to, but I liked the way you approached and I played along. Don't think you fooled me".

Sudhir was growing in stature and was getting acknowledged for his competency in conducting interviews which were very popular in Maharashtra. Noted singers like Lata Mangeshkar and Asha Bhonsle always wanted Sudhir to anchor their shows and very soon he became close enough to address them as "Didi" (elder sister). He was part of a large number of programs held abroad. During one of his foreign tours, he met Mr Choughule of Choughule wines. During the discussion, he expressed unhappiness about the fact that he had to leave his parents behind in Kolhapur and he missed seeing them. Sudhir offered to make a short film of his parents. This set in motion a whole new trend of making films of loved ones back in India. When Sudhir showed the film to Choughule, he had tears in his eyes. What started as single film soon became a trend and Sudhir made 120 such films. Such was the acclaim that Times of India carried an article titled "Packaging Grand Pa" after he completed 50 films.

Sudhir is a firm believer that the interviewer has a larger role to play. More so, when the person is well known and is popular in public domain. It should not be the endeavor to show him/her down but to showcase them well. Only cases of crime and corruption need to be dealt strongly devoid of compassion.

Once, while conducting a live interview of Madhuri Dixit, the legendary beauty and heroine, he asked her to sing, since he knew she could sing; a fact not known to many. She agreed and sang and very soon the song became very popular. Thus, Sudhir showcased the strength of the most sought after heroine which was largely unknown in the public domain and presenting a positive side in the interview.

Sudhir is fearless and undaunted. He spares no one and is benign to none. His interviews reflect a very high degree of impartiality and conviction. While interviewing political bigwigs, he can adopt an ice cold demeanor with direct questions on flaws and contradictions they so often represent. He never hesitated to put in dock any person he found to be of questionable propriety. Such was his influence that he could establish a personal rapport with many a high dignitaries. He proudly shows his pictures sitting next to the then President APJ Abdul Kalaam, a privilege reserved exclusively for the PM, Governors or the CM's.

Dare to Dream

He concedes that the road to success has been very tough and hard. He credits his value system acquired from his parents and family as the fundamental reason for his survival. How could he tackle politics, politicians and political pressures? His answer is very simple. "During my career spanning decades, I came in contact with a lot of influential people and leaders. One thing was clear, I maintained foolproof integrity, never sought personal favors for me, my family or friends. Never used this position of influence to my personal advantage. This gives me confidence to look straight into the eyes of those I interview and ask questions without fear or favor".

What then are the traits that are needed to be a good journalist and achieve success akin to his? He cautions "There are few attributes which are very demanding in this profession. One has to be prepared to work very hard in tough conditions for a long time; one needs to study, prepare and understand a lot. Characteristics like integrity and honesty have a greater import, time is of immense significance, develop the quality of mental agility to deal with impromptu situations, be physically fit and emotionally strong and finally develop the quality of objectivity devoid of bias".

Modern day journalism has undergone a sea change. Influx of technology has made reporting and responding, real time. With the increasing number of TV channels, news has become more of competitive reporting rather than qualitative reporting. The shift to 24 hour channels has lead to chasing stories that have sensational value and not reporting value. Internet proliferation has encroached upon the traditional print mediums and has put a question mark on their future. Though these are inevitable changes, Sudhir feels, adaptation and adjustments will take place in due course of time and in the end it is quality that will prevail. The basic tenets of journalism with respect to reporting standards, integrity and realism shall never be overtaken by avaricious news channel, sites or papers looking to make a kill. Sudhir feels technology cannot replace journalism as technology is an enabler or the medium of dispersal and not the medium of expression. In this context, at the heart of every endeavor remains the one person who cannot be replaced; the journalist.

Sudhir looks back with pride and looks ahead with curiosity and enthusiasm. A lot more needs to be done and a lot more can be expected. As a journalist, his questions can never cease and he remains what he always wants to be and what he likes to be "A Passionate Interlocutor" probing forever for probity in public life.

■ ■ ■

Key Learning Values

Adjustment and Accommodation: In order to maintain relationships on a long term, the need for adjustment and accommodation must be understood. This would be significant in both work and personal life.

Art of Deliberations: Understanding the nuances of deliberations is the key to successful discussions and decisions. Effective deliberations also lead to better compliance.

Keen Sense of Observation: Observation is the foundation of understanding. As said" Seeing is believing". In any profession visual understanding and correct visualization always play a key role in analyzing any situation.

Pursuing Passion with Perseverance: Once the nature of work and passion are blended together, there should be no stopping. All out effort must become a habit.

Integrity and Propriety: Personal and organizational branding and reputation are closely linked with integrity and propriety. These demonstrated values add immense goodwill at all times.

Communicating with Commitment: Communication must be meaningful, accurate, timely and specific.

Dr. Anand Deshpande

Success is possible only when one is able to identify what one can do and do it the best. Have clarity of needed competencies and work to strengthen them. Choose your direction and pursue vigorously with focus.

VISION TO ENVISION

Dr. Anand Deshpande

Blissful Yet Conscious

Growing up is always an important phase in a child's life and it usually defines many a future characteristics. For a child in a township, like the one in which Anand was brought up, the experience was quite unique. Anand's father, was an engineer, employed with Bharat Heavy Electricals Limited (BHEL) in Bhopal; one the few PSU's known for being profitable. The township was huge and accommodated around 25000 people. Such townships are usually located away from the main stream of the city and are self contained with social interaction becoming inclusive and focused inwards. Adequate spaces, parks, playgrounds, markets and recreational facilities with in such townships insulate them to a great extent from the local influences. In many ways, these townships develop a distinctiveness of their own retaining a national character and a cosmopolitan flavor.

For Anand, childhood growing up experience is more like being among equals. Neighbors had a similar status, the houses were identical, financial status and lifestyle was comparable, the means of entertainment was alike and children went to similar schools and even aspired for similar things. Neighbors and friends being from different parts of the country, a child in such environs, grew up learning to live with more ease. Festivals are celebrated together and social interaction enabled understanding and accepting cross culture effortlessly. While such township experiences were rewarding, one thing was uniquely common. Anand explains "The environment in our township was study centric; it was inevitable as most parents would tell their children that doing well in studies was the only way to succeed". There was a lot of play and fun but the bottom lines were very clearly drawn and the priorities very clear with expectations spelt out in no uncertain terms that one had to do well in studies. In a background where future greatly depended on how well one would do in studies, he found his focus no different from others.

While growing up is always a blissful age, there was a constant remainder resonating not just from home but also from the community he lived which made him conscious of the fact that study was indeed, the call of the day. These years at the township subconsciously infused a sense of purpose and made Anand aware of the importance of learning.

Academic Journey

Anand was a serious student. He took academics to heart and worked hard. Though he would take active part in many activities, he would purposefully ensure that such activities did not compromise his academic performance. He would do his home work in time, prepare for his classes and do well in his exams. Anand recalls "I was a very good student and always did everything that was expected out of me. I felt that there was a lot of competitive pressure from my friends because everyone was quite focused. I had no choice as the prevailing ambience ensured academic rigor". As a good student with diligent habits and good performance, he was always encouraged by his teachers. Even today, he says, with a tinge of pride that his teachers remember him well.

As expected, he opted for the Physics, Chemistry and Mathematics combination in high school. He was also a National Science Talent Search Merit Scholarship holder; an achievement which was very creditable considering the number of students who aim for it. He had his aim clear that the next course to pursue was engineering. Anand says "I was never compelled by anyone to opt for engineering. It was my decision as I wanted to be an engineer, like my father".

On successfully completing his HSC, he appeared for Joint Entrance Examination for admission to the IIT's and was successful in qualifying, resulting in his admission at IIT Kharagpur. His position in the overall merit earned him a scholarship at IIT too. He joined Aeronautical Engineering as his specialization. However, he found things to be different. Different in the sense that students were very intelligent, studious and focused, very competitive and self motivated. Professors were highly qualified and committed. They were fully involved with their job and were seized with their responsibilities. It was a sea change in approach, which Anand experienced; in teaching methods, learning environment and overall commitment. Anand was never daunted by challenges; they just added fuel to fire his own motivation.

After the second year at IIT, the institute introduced Computer Science as a new domain and threw open to his batch. There were just 20 seats and students after II year were permitted to apply. The selection was to be made purely on merit, based on the grades and performance. A large number of students wanted to opt for computer science as it was considered the most emerging area with tremendous scope and opportunity. Anand applied and found his name in the top twenty. This is a major turning point in his career as this choice, in years to come, would showcase not just his technical capabilities but also his entrepreneurial skills. By 1984, he completed B. Tech (Computer Science) and the next option was to be exercised.

"It was something everybody who secured good grades did those days; applying to US universities for Post Graduation/ PhD. So did I and secured admission to a Five Year Integrated PhD Program at Indiana University USA, with a scholarship and I took it". This became a very significant event which shaped the way future would unfold.

The experience at Indiana University was amazing. It proved to be totally different from the atmosphere he experienced at IIT. At IIT, the teaching methods were traditional top driven mode, students did not have much fiexibility of what they wish to choose as subjects, the program was highly exam and mark centric. In comparison, he was exposed to a more stimulating environment. At Indiana, the teaching was more supportive than directive, students were expected to read, learn and participate by way of discussions in class, there was a greater choice of subjects and options with students, more flexible assessment, less dependent on exam pattern and one that inspired freedom of thought and expression. Anand found this new system exciting and went about it with renewed enthusiasm.

One thing was always constant with Anand and that was hard work and consistency. Whether it was school, IIT or Indiana University, it was this attribute that enabled him to standout. By the end of first year, he performed so well so as make him eligible for admission to the remainder program for PhD. This was a significant achievement and not an easy one at that, though, he makes it feel so.

At this juncture, he was allotted a mentor who was to be his guide for PhD. His mentor was just a few years older and Anand was his first PhD research scholar. Anand felt very much at ease with his guide and together they did a lot of work by way of publishing papers, attending seminars, doing joint projects and writing to scientific journals of repute. Under his guidance, Anand was able to secure his PhD successfully by the end of five years specializing in data base management systems. On completion of PhD, he applied for a job at Hewlett-Packard (HP) and was absorbed at their parent facility at Paulo Alto.

A Call from Within

To most Indians who go abroad for higher studies, the next destination in mind would be to secure a well paying job in a company of repute. For Anand, it seemed quite like a "fait accompli"; PhD from a university of repute, followed by a job in company known worldwide. Things seemed too perfect and well set for a young Indian looking for a worthwhile career. For Anand, something rankled within, he was there in USA physically but the soul elsewhere. It did not need much to decide what he did. While most looked at that decision with lot of skepticism, he still took the call. He did what his heart wanted him to do and the call from within beckoned him back to India.

It was indeed a tough decision; leaving a well paid job, in a company of repute and in the domain of choice. The alternatives were least impressive, yet the desire to create a business by himself, a feeling of a need to do something, a strong network abroad, drove him to entrepreneurship in the form starting a company aptly named as "Persistent" symbolizing a will to seek, survive and sustain. This was major decision of immense significance which made all the change. It was probably the impact of the values imbibed due to his upbringing which attracted him back to his roots.

Road to Success

Getting back to India with a strong passion is one thing and actually starting a software business was another. India was a land of hurdles and has the ability to take out every iota of patriotic instincts from those who return with a dream. Early,1990's were not very ideal for a technology driven business and India was not looked upon as an ideal software destination. There were basic issues such as rudimentary telecommunications, limited access to internet, difficulty in real time communications, issues with export/import regulations, aspects of foreign exchange, to name a few. There were also numerous administrative regulations to be complied. It needed more than "Persistence" and patience to persevere this situation and prevail. Despite all these challenges "Persistent" became a reality in 1992.

Initial years were very tough and business was hard to come by. The networking and relation building quality of Anand stood up to his advantage and began to pay dividends. Anand also chose the correct domain to operate i.e. database management, which was his strength and an area which was getting to be significant at that time. His contacts in USA enabled him to bag initial contracts; though not very huge, they became the foundation for growth as time rolled by. By 1996, things began to change as the policy of the government got more aligned to liberalization, globalization and privatization. The focus shifted towards enhancing and improving technical infrastructure and with this came the swing to propel the fortunes of the company.

Having spent initial years in embedding themselves, Persistent was beginning to get acknowledged in India and abroad. How does a company of this nature grow and how do customers get to know? Anand explains "This is a business which is network centric. One must understand the term networking is not just building relationship but building trustworthy professional performance oriented relationship. Word of mouth, references and reputation play a very significant part". He maintains that delivery execution and post delivery support to the customer as very essential. Both the company and customer should realize that in software business there could be many post delivery glitches. The company should take ownership and ensure these problems are settled by displaying a sense of affiliation. The blame game approach never works especially in technology and intellectually driven businesses. One dissatisfied customer can do more damage than 10 good customers.

Persistent today stands tall on the landscape of IT Companies and Anand can proudly feel the pleasure of hard work and dedication bearing fruit. A dream comes true!

As a leader, how challenging was this journey, what difficulties did he face in and how the work life balance could be achieved?

Anand tells it all "A journey of this nature has to have its share of challenges. One has deal with each one the as they come by. We started small taking small jobs and operating in small teams. We focused only on what we can do well and what we can deliver with excellence. This helped in positioning ourselves as an organization with a focus on delivery with accuracy. As we began to grow, so did our teams and level of work. Software being an intellectually driven activity in groups, one had to ensure compatibility, freedom, fiexibility and accountability".

Whether you manage a sports team or an IT team, the outcome is always on the result. It is therefore very important to create this awareness and make people aligned to the company vision of delivery and excellence. Teams are handpicked and nominated with specific goals and targets and this resulted in Persistent meeting customer needs effectively. Innovation and keeping pace with technology becomes second nature and continuous learning and upgrading a necessity. Constant market surveillance and customer feedback as regards their changing needs, plays an important role in identifying new areas of work.

Anand feels that the concept of work life balance needs a relook. It is his belief, that both are inseparable and cannot be delinked. Neither one can walk away from work nor can continue always and all the time. It is matter of priority which determines which must take precedence when. The best way is to figure out a way to work and live together and accept work with joy.

Reflections

Persistent System has over 8000 employees and is spread over three continents with facilities over 20 locations world over. It occupies a position of prestige and trust. Having achieved success, he feels that the basic secret was identifying correctly what he can do and doing it well. He was always very clear about the competencies to be strengthened. He is a firm believer of the fact that one can never ride two horses at one time. This enabled him to develop specific core competencies which ensured the company remained in reckoning.

The way the company started with database management and then gradually realigned itself to the emerging areas like cloud computing and analytics is an apt example. This he feels is a major takeaway and would like the younger generation to identify and strengthen their strengths.

He now looks at making a change and doing something that eventually have a great social impact. Being an entrepreneur, he realizes that the greatest challenge that awaits India is creating employment. The demographic dividend that one speaks will be of no avail if job creation fails to keep pace. It is with this purpose, he has now begun to focus on job creation through his foundation which has a substantial amount of his personal resources and time committed to it. It is his passionate dream to create entrepreneurs from young people emerging out of ITI's and equip them with training and wear withal including finance and mentorial support. He looks at being able to create 25000 such entrepreneurs who in turn would create a large number of jobs; something the nation needs. This is his major dream for future.

Anand has time on his side, still young enough to be at the helm for many decades to come, he can truly make things happen the way he sees them. He is not just someone, who has a "Vision to Envision" but is one who has the ability to transform "Envisioned Vision" to a reality.

■ ■ ■

Key Learning Values

Focus and Direction: This attribute greatly helps in enabling consistent performance, Earlier an individual identifies his focus, better will be the journey to success.

Hard work with Diligence: Imply identifying an area of interest may not be focus. Unless it is coupled with hard work and diligence, doors of success may not open.

Clarity of Thought: This is a very important value. What to do, how to do and more importantly when to do are the outcomes of a clear mind. Clarity gives the correct direction and even propulsion to one's aims.

Vigorous Pursuit: Once a decision has been made, there should be no looking back.

Contribution to Larger Good: The objective of earning should always result in larger good. Good organizations invest a lot on public service. True service is not lip service but demonstrated action.

Shantilal Muttha

"Changes in social practices can happen only by proving efficacy of alternative solutions. Demonstrate change by personal example not just by words".

A MONOLITH: ALONE BUT NEVER LONELY

Shantilal Muttha

An Early Revelation

For a ten year old boy, it was an unusual experience. Born in a small town in a very modest family, the child had to be sent to a charitable hostel which subsisted on donations from the affluent Jain community. It was a custom those days for the boys from the hostel to serve meals to guests at weddings and social events of the community on whose support the hostel relied on. Functions were elaborate and to a young boy, the contrasts were very striking. The glaring dissimilarities he saw between opulence and depravation, wealthy and not so wealthy, made him ponder. This picture of contrast was imprinted not only on his mind but left a mark on his emotions and heart cementing in place a thought; an action and a future vision of working towards greater harmony between the haves and the have not's.

These early experiences were not only challenging for young Shantilal, but proved to be enriching. Recalling those days "Serving people and observing their affluence and social arrogance gave me an instinctive understanding of human nature. I started to believe that something needs to be done to set right the aspects of social disparity. I was exposed to the need to remain humble in best or worse situations". Early impressions became the foundation for engineering socially active thoughts which in later years manifested as actions in very many ways.

These experiences strengthened the belief that education was necessary to find solutions to address social issues. Though, he was not so enthused about education and learning, he realized that acquiring qualifications and exploring the city culture was imperative. It was a prerequisite to get the support of his family to seek a new direction since his family expected him to join his father's grocery business on completion of schooling. For Shantilal, horizons lay beyond managing a grocery shop, he was cut out for something exclusive. It is this self-belief that convinced his father and very soon, he was on his way to Ahmednagar for XII class and to Pune subsequently for graduation.

His modest background, limited resources and exposure did not deter Shantilal who was a keen observer, a willing learner and a passionate believer in himself. It was this self-discovery which emboldened him to embark on an uncharted course. Circumstances in his early childhood did not brow beat him to submission and acceptance of fate and destiny. *He wanted to be different not because difference mattered but because he wanted to make a difference to many.* These early value indicators would find an imprint in the way he navigated his future.

Activist and Activism to Alternatives

Years at Pune posed a huge challenge. Coming from a rural background, the sudden change to city culture, language, habits, dress and lifestyle was a daunting experience. Undeterred Shantilal accepted these challenges in his stride, never letting what he did not possess overpower what he did. He worked to earn, engaged in service activities, improved his circle of friends and found a renewed sense of confidence as he explored new areas like social activism to focus on relevant social issues of significance.

It was during this time, his first major lesson was driven home. Around late 1970's, he along with his friend led a protest against an unabashed display of wealth at a wedding ceremony of the daughter of a well-known industrialist. As they protested, the industrialist met Shantilal and told him "It's my money and I can spend it the way I like and others have no right to interfere". These words symbolized that side of the society which was not only resistant but also preventive of change. This incident highlighted to Shantilal the need to identify and address problems and find alternatives. He realized that change cannot happen by activism, it has to happen by demonstrated actions offering solutions. It set in motion a new thinking that called for persistent and sustained action.

A Career on the Rise

Shantilal understood that to create alternative solution to social ills, resources were necessary. To do so, he ventured into entrepreneurship by choosing real estate business. A very significant decision considering that neither Shantilal had experience nor was he a qualified engineer. He dared to tread this path only because he saw an opportunity and put all his reputation at stake. It was early 80's, and this represented a very right time and a right opportunity. Seizing this chance with open arms, Shantilal moved on from being a real estate broker to realty developer. Success embraced and the ventures were successful.

The unique reason for this success as a developer was his focus on *three path breaking attributes; Firstly, Construction with quality, Secondly, affordable price and thirdly, commitment and value to customer.* In retrospect, this was a huge achievement because for a rural boy to seek challenges in city, enter social activism, understand the psyche of the society and create a value centric real estate success, the story was simply astounding. "A fairy tale in making". Shantilal recounts humbly *"It is risk taking, zeal, perseverance, grit, goodwill and blessings of god almighty which enabled success".*

Standing Firm for a Dream

With success comes name and acknowledgment and people crave for more and expand further. Shantilal decided to deviate from the norms of business. Instead of finding ways to enlarge, expand and earn, he decided to call it quits. His decision to leave business was spurred by his ideas for contributing towards bringing about a social change. Shantilal was subjected to severe pressure from all quarters including his immediate family to drop this idea and focus on business. *Exiting from the existing successful business model to work for the society at the young age of 31 was simply "Unthinkable". People become great because they convert the unthinkable into thinkable and take extraordinary decisions to fulfill their dreams.* The creation of Bharatiya Jain Sanghatan (BJS) thus became a reality rising out of the dream of dreamer who envisaged contribution to make a better new world.

Post 1986 … Picking Up The Gauntlet

Shantilal was rearing to go, energy abound, he knew with time, age and resources on his side, it was time to fly. He decided to focus on three core issues which were close to his heart. First, tackling female exploitative practices such as, dowry system, female feticide and Illiteracy: the second was to educate the masses especially the rural population regarding the imbalanced and skewed male versus female sex ratio and thirdly the curtailment of exorbitant wedding expenditures. Adopting a unique approach, Shantilal undertook 3000 km padayatra across Maharashtra with sole purpose of reaching out and sensitizing masses on the need to accept changing realities. He made a conscious decision not to criticize the existing traditional practices but offer acceptable alternative solutions which would facilitate greater acceptance. His alternatives such as "Mass Marriages, Vadhu-Var Parichay Sammelans were a great success. These paved way in generating a positive change in mindset towards the existing practices and made people more amenable in the face of obvious benefits such as lower cost of marriage, reduction in dowry and even address the declining female ratio. By conducting the marriage of his son and daughter at mass marriage ritual, Shantilal demonstrated his belief in word and action as a true leader. Across Maharashtra mass marriages gained substantial acceptability.

As time progressed, Shantilal expanded his sphere of operations to include a varied socially relevant and community centric projects. He envisaged a greater role for organizations like *BJS* in ensuring a responsible role in communally sensitive areas and was instrumental in containing a surcharged atmosphere post demolition of Babri Masjid. *BJS* also initiated itself into Disaster Management in a big way and was seen contributing hand in hand with governments in affected areas from its own resources. Rehabilitation post riots, educational rehabilitation to include school quality improvement and enhancement, floods, tsunami, earthquakes which inflicted losses of life and property, became the area of expertise. Rehabilitation and resettlement of communities and children became an area of focus. Throughout the decade from 2000 onwards, India was subjected numerous natural disasters and Shantilal with his dedicated team were omnipresent to deal with these disasters with efficiency and effectiveness. Consistent and with utmost involvement, the team BJS under Shantilal has tirelessly and ceaselessly worked in over 14 major disasters. A man with a keen sense of perception, Shantilal during his activities observed that our education system was more systemic than value driven. For these to evolve, it was essential that focus be shifted towards identifying and implementing value driven programs at school level. This led to evolution and birth of EDUQUIP. This unique educational mission is intended to focus on adding values and culture to education through introduction of values into the system and creating quantifiable evaluation based activities. The intention of Shantilal has been two fold; firstly to enhance the quality and enable overall improvement in standards and secondly, to create an atmosphere of values to shape the character.

As years passed by; Business houses across the country expanded and diversified into multiple businesses for profit, where as Shantilal diversified and expanded into multiple social verticals for benefit. His footprint was substantial encompassing Education, Mission against Social Evils, Female Empowerment, Entrepreneurship Development, Student Assessment Programs and Career Development, Focus on School Development, Accreditation, Disaster Management in all forms. Looking back… How does he feel his contribution will be recalled in years to come; Shantilal explained that he likens himself to the sparrow who attempted to fight a forest fire.

A huge fire raged in a jungle and all the animals and birds began to flee to safety. As the fire increased in intensity, a group of crows who were making a racket with their cawing sounds observed something unusual. A small sparrow was ferrying water in its beak and was dropping those droplets in to the raging fire. Repeatedly without rest it would make trip after trip and was at the point of exhaustion. One elderly crow followed the sparrow and said" Stupid bird! Why are you so foolish.. Don't you know that with these few drops of water from your beak you can never fight the fire: if you continue you will soon be burned to death" The sparrow replied "Brother, when the story of this fire is written, I would like to be remembered as the one who tried to fight the fire and not as one who took off in a flight away from fire"

To Shantilal, his mission has no end, he knows he has just begun and he knows he must walk and stand firm. Dealing with problems so large is like dealing with a forest fire. Yet, undeterred, like the sparrow, he must continue. As he looks out of the top floor office at the setting sun on the horizon; He knows the boundary is beyond, like a monolith, he must stand firm, withstand the vagaries of the society stoically and move on...

Alone but never lonely as what he does touches lives and hearts of many.

■ ■ ■

Key Personality Attributes

Face the Reality: Understanding situations as they exist and evaluating them objectively to arrive at solutions rather than confrontation.

Patience: Every action initiated to bring about a change will require a lot of patience. Changing mind sets is difficult but changing habits may be easier. Long haul requires patience in dealing, execution and expectation.

Persistence: A never say die attitude is essential to pursue any goal in life.

Pragmatism: It's the ability of self belief which needs to be undying, consistent and continuous. A pragmatic approach will always result in solution centric thinking rather than mere activist modes which may result in confrontation.

Persuasion: Ability to convince people by right expression rather than by compulsion or through incentivisation.

Positivity: Any mission with zeal will involve hurdles, obstacles and difficulties. As one clears many others open. Challenges and conflicts will be many. Positive attitude will always help in solving crisis and forging ahead.

Dr. Shriram Lagoo

When the call is from with in, change must happen. Risk becomes Inconsequential. You have to do because you need to do. So go for it when you seek it from your heart.

A CHOICE BEYOND REASON

Dr. Shriram Lagoo

A Square Peg in a Round Hole

One of the most difficult decisions a young student faces is making a choice of career and the options to choose. Pursue passion, do whatever the heart says; many such words of advice seem to be redundant to a growing mind which tends to lean on many factors. There is always a confusion always between what one likes to do and what one is expected to do. At a young age, it becomes quite a challenging decision and it is but natural for young men and women to lean on their parents to seek a direction for further education. This has been a dilemma in the past, remains a dilemma today and shall be a dilemma tomorrow. In the Indian context, intelligence, performance and choice of career are very closely linked. Professions like medicine and engineering have been traditionally considered as the options for the bright. "Good" students had no choice and "good" parents had no other expectation and invariably whether one wanted or not, most students who do well in school customarily found themselves in one of the two; ending up as engineers or doctors more by default than design.

After he completed his schooling, Shriram too was in a similar dilemma. His father was a fairly well established doctor and it was thus expected that he would take up medicine in his father's footsteps. This was the most natural thing expected to happen. No one asked him and no one even thought that he could be nursing a different dream. To some extent, it would have been abominable to think differently even for a second. Doctor's son! What else can he be! other than be a doctor and take the legacy ahead.

Inadvertently, Shriram found himself enrolled to the medical program and joined the very first batch of MBBS at the BJ Medical College, Pune. Thus Shriram joined medical college not so much by choice but because of expectation. He never really had an option to think and deliberate. He did what was told as good for him. His father was very eager to see him complete his medical course and take over the responsibility of managing the clinic thereby enabling him to devote full time for active politics.

Many years down the line, Shriram had earned a lot of name and fame and he stands tall as a revered figure; not in the field of medicine but in the field of cinema and drama as an actor par excellence. When seen from the point it started and the way it navigated; the divergence in the journey is distinctly different. In many ways, proving the initial choice seem as "A square peg in a round hole".

Face to Face with Greats

Growing years are always the best. Carefree and unbridled for a child, family, friends and the seamless intimacies add charm to childhood. Shriram grew up in comfortable environs enjoying the best of everything. Dr. BC Lagoo, his father, in addition to being a medical practitioner, was a well known political figure. He was a member of the Congress party and was having a position of eminence in the party hierarchy. He was intimately involved with activities of the Congress in the pre independent India. In 1940's, a lot was happening and Pune was a crucible for many an event related to the independence struggle. Shriram was fortunate to have a ringside view of the growing momentum of the independence struggle. These were the most important times of history as a lot was about to happen. Children of his age had be part of this surge and get overwhelmed by the patriotic swing and mood of the nation.

For Shriram, the experiences were terrific. He recalls "I very vividly remember the excitement when I used to hear stalwart leaders like Mahatma Gandhi, Pandit Jawaharlal Nehru. Dr. C. Rajagopalachary, arriving and staying at our house. We would wait expectantly for these leaders to arrive and then meet and greet them by touching their feet". To Shriram, meeting leaders of such caliber and briefly interacting with them gave him immense confidence and a great feeling of patriotism. Observing these leaders at such close quarters and seeing their work style, instilled in Shriram, the importance of continuos and untiring effort.

Shriram recalls "It is quite unimaginable to be able to see such towering personalities in real life. To me, the very fact that they visited and stayed in our house was a source of immense pride and motivation". His father being a very senior functionary, it was but natural for the leaders of the congress party to be at Shriram's house during their visits. Shriram recollects the unending energy, never ending patience, continuous communication, humility and humbleness, willingness to meet people as some of the significant attributes displayed in abundance by these leaders. He remembers sitting on the stair case of their two floor bungalow, the day he saw Jawaharlal Nehru. He came after a long and a tiring day. "I saw him come in as breezily as if the day had just begun, cheerful, smiling and greeting, he patted me and moved up the staircase not the way people usually do; climbing one step at a time holding the railing but literally jumping by stepping over two steps at a time". What amazed me was the energy, enthusiasm and untiring spirit he demonstrated by that action. He spoke nothing but said a lot; such images remained with me all through my life". He recalls the distinctive aura which surrounded the Mahatma; seeing him personally in his house was possibly Shriram's greatest moment in life. As he bowed down to touch his feet to seek his blessings, Shriram remembers the exhilaration as Mahatma's hand touched his forehead gently and the words resonated "Whatever you do, be sure to be right in doing so". Undoubtedly, Shriram was very fortunate to have grown up in the shadow of legends.

Growing up in that politically surcharged environment added to his awareness and understanding. His father had a lucrative private practice but he was thoroughly involved and committed to the freedom struggle. He was not the one who looked for personal achievements in the organization but was a contributor who believed in doing the best for the good of the organization. His father's selfless approach taught Shriram the very important lesson of giving everything with full spirit once a commitment is made. Once you make a choice, the only choice is to give it all.

Walking Along

As a student in school, Shriram was just above the average. He was not one of those his friends and teachers felt as scholastic or intelligent but on the contrary, he was neither dull nor the one who lagged behind. He attended classes, appeared in exams and passed all of them always in time, never a failure but never a topper. Though he was growing up in a household which was in the forefront from a political perspective, he never developed any inclination towards politics. Joint family in pre independent India was a social norm. It was an expectation in the society and every family be a joint family. To that extent, his father being the eldest presided over the family which consisted of his four brothers and two sisters. Like most who grew up in these environs, Shriram too was a part and parcel of the joint family culture which propagated community living. In other words, the biggest lesson for him was "One for all and all for one". Everything should belong to everybody and everybody will do everything for everybody. His family was fairly well to do, though they did not suffer from the tribulations of scarce living, it was a shared living. This growing up phase for Shriram was instrumental in giving him resilience to withstand pressures and ability to deal with issues through adjustment.

During his school days, Shriram never really demonstrated anything special. Though, he did show an inclination towards drama, it did not manifest in any definite form. Post school, he joined Fergusson College and the two years spent there before joining the medical college did show some sparks of theatre and drama as the seed seems to have been sown. The choice of entering the medical college was that of his father. At that time, even Shriram never really gave it a thought whether that was what he actually wanted to do. His father expected him to take medicine and he simply complied. Medical college was a revelation of sorts for Shriram. He was regular, consistent and worked to the best of his ability. It was here, he got the real exposure and opportunity to test his inner love for drama. His first performance came at the Annual College day and he was highly inspired by the response of his friends and teachers. He felt the pleasure of emoting on stage and this craving soon became an intense desire. Throughout the five year stint at the medical college, Shriram seized every possible opportunity to be on stage, acting in plays and dramas. This gave him immense confidence and cemented his first love which was so far hidden within himself.

Shriram also credits his professors and friends who encouraged his talent during his medical college days. Unlike other professional colleges where the focus is just on academics, at BJ Medical College, the exposure he received and the support he garnered was the turning point in his life which enabled him to think in a different direction in days to come. During his college days, a distant relative who was an Assistant Director, in films was staying with them. As the age difference between them was not much, they became friends and through him, Shriram began to learn a lot about film making and this stirred in him a desire to be on screen and be known as an actor. Such was his passion within, that he would watch a movie and come home and try to enact the role which he liked most.

On completion of his MBBS, he was expected to take over the private practice set up by his father. Shriram did so in deference to his father's wishes and managed the clinic well. In the years to come, he realized that, being a general practitioner like his father was not something he wanted and went on to do his specialization in ENT (Ear Nose and Throat). Soon from general medicine, he graduated to specialization and it appeared that the medical profession was all set to take off and the dream of being on stage and screen seemed too remote to be a reality.

From Doctor to an Actor

Shriram's romance and inclination for drama was well entrenched. It was too deep to be unsettled. As he began to settle down in medical profession, he ensured that his heart's passion was not ignored. He began to take active interest in dramas and took part in acting. To him acting in a good role was more important than being acknowledged for a specific role. He took upon himself, to study, prepare and understand the character he would portray. To him, every play and every role was like his first role and never did he ever look down on preparation.

Soon it became obvious, that he could no longer ride two horses at the same time and the moment had come to make a choice. He was married, well settled in medical profession, had a good family background, was carrying forward his father's name and legacy and was well respected and acknowledged. There was possibly no one who would advice him to leave his medical practice at this juncture to pursue what appeared like a day dream to many and even a nightmare to some. In those days, the profession of acting was fine but it was not something respectable people from respectable families were expected to take up. Shriram was in a true dilemma; his heart was not in what he was doing and what his heart wanted was not what everyone wanted. When one is at a threshold of such a decision, it is but natural to weather opposition. His father left the decision to him and Shriram had the backing of his wife who stood and rallied around him. It was a love marriage and in true spirit of love, she became his support system and encouraged him to do what he wanted in life. Thus came the turning point. At the first opportune moment, Shriram bid goodbye to medicine and took up acting professionally.

What began as a trickle soon became a flood of opportunity. His talent, commitment and intensity earned him a good name and made him the most sought after character actor. Did he never aspire to be a hero? Shriram says "To me the diversity of roles was more important. I was never interested in getting branded as a hero or a villain. This gave me a greater opportunity to showcase my talent and meet my dream of being an actor". He became a name to be reckoned with and very soon became a familiar face in Hindi and Marathi cinema. Though a late starter, his rise had been no less phenomenal.

Was it a very tough call, to drop a prospering medical practice after 10 years and enter a career which was totally an ambiguity with no guarantee of success? Shriram reflects, "No doubt, it was a difficult decision. The issue is when one starts to feel vegetated in the profession one is, and the heart is calling out for a change, risk becomes inconsequential. You want to go because you want to be there. You seek a change because you love the change and you want to be part of it and it has no limits defined. I wanted to be an actor and that was the intense passion; no more no less". He would choose only those roles which were stimulating and the stories inspiring. He never considered remuneration as a means to choose or reject a role. He was always a believer that it is not the role but how well one lives in the role that makes it good. To have achieved such reputation for excellence is no mean achievement. What could be the factors which influenced this success? Shriram explains "Few important traits that helped me were, having complete knowledge of the role, being versatile, having a strong conviction, flair for acting, a professional approach in terms of behavior and conduct, unwavering commitment and choosing only those roles which impress". Shriram always believed in spectator feedback on his performances as he was convinced that they were the right ones to judge and not the critics or experts. Shriram also reiterates that in today's world of options and choices, the younger generation should never be compelled to choose.

Free hand must be given to them to choose a profession of choice as the profession of their livelihood. His words for the young are very simple and straight "Do whatever you want to do but when you do so do it as if your life depended on it. Never ever do anything half hearted as half effort is more dangerous than no effort". To the parents of today, he just says "do not force the younger generation to do what they don't like because forcing them to do is something unfortunate". It is said, "stars never fade". They remain forever in the sky and glimmer at night reminding us of the beauty of their glow. An actor's life is so much akin to that of a star; glowing for others, glittering to give joy and in the bargain someday remain twinkling amongst many always visible but yet obscure.

Shriram's life is a unique success story and proves that every choice need not have reason and every reason need not have a choice. At best, even a "Choice Beyond Reason" can be a reason to succeed.

■ ■ ■

Key Learning Values

Anytime is Right Time: If choice has to be made, it must be made. Never let go thinking it is too late to begin.

Firm in Resolve: Once a decision is made to begin, the resolve must be firm and there should be no re think .

Self Discipline: If one has to pursue passion as a profession, self discipline is a must. Success or failure is greatly dependent on this.

Adherence to Commitment: A total adherence to do what one decides to do. Difficulties can be overcome if commitment is total.

Effort Must Be Complete: The ultimate answer to be what you wish to be is the effort that goes into doing it.

Dr. Balaji Tambe

Modernity is not opposing the legacy of tradition but accepting change. Modernity is not refusing to do but adapting to times. Flexibility in thought, maturity in understanding and willingness to be different are the key attributes needed to bring about a change in behavior.

SCRIPTING
THE IMPROBABLE

Dr. Balaji Tambe

In Deference to Difference

Well beyond the city limits, away from the din and glare of the evolving city of Pune, like an oasis, in the middle of nowhere, is the compact ashram of Shreeguru Balaji Tambe. To an inquisitive outsider, it may look more like a resort, as it breaks the mould of a traditional ashram. Nestled in the midst of greenery and tranquil sounds of nature, the ashram, houses a capacity of 150 guests, who come from India and the world over to get treated for their physical and emotional ailments through Ayurveda and a spiritual experience of a different kind. A Skeptic may imprudently brush it aside as just one those gimmicks to get people hooked onto the traditional Indian methods purely for business. How did Balaji who grow up in the household atmosphere of Vedas, Scriptures and Ayurvedic traditions decide to become an engineer? Even more surprising, how did an engineer, who started his career in industry end up being an exponent of Ayurveda and spiritual healing? What is it that attracted him to make a contribution to this field not from the view point of business but more from the point view of service? How did this happen and what prompted him to be the one to show deference to be the difference?

It is very common to see, when people are unaware of something, they get wary and suspicious; when they are ignorant, they avoid or discard. Complex as it is, a country like India with its diversity, poses great hurdles, as less literate tend to be superstitious and the educated gravitate towards disbelief. The net result is, most Indian scientific traditional applications like Yoga, Ayurveda, Astrology get associated with religion and thus get insulated from mainstream.

Balaji was all set to be different because he believed that mere deference or acceptance by him would not suffice and he must step in to this arena and find ways to make this mission of bringing the Indian thoughts and traditional methods back to mainstream and resuscitate the long lost Vedic knowledge for quality lifestyle. Thus began a long distinctive journey of moving beyond the predefined path.

Predestined to Begin

It is quite an astounding assertion and one which leaves you in awe. Balaji says *"My entry into this world is predetermined with defined task to do"*. *He further adds, "I actually chose my parents"* and thus was born to Vasudev Tambe Shastri and Lakshmibai. His father was acknowledged as one of those who has achieved a very high level of spiritual knowledge and was respected for his pious life style. Balaji was exposed to a very stringent regime of spiritual education from his childhood. His father was a strict disciplinarian, who insisted and expected a very set of behavior norms from his children. The day used to start early with exercise, yoga and followed by spiritual education in a very formal way. His father was a great Sanskrit scholar and knew the entire Rigveda by heart. He was an example of piety, commitment to spirituality and austerity through self imposed guidelines for a disciplined life. Balaji was always attracted to spiritual and abstract worlds. It is this inner call that created inquisitiveness in that sphere. The atmosphere at home was very conducive to the study of Vedas, Upanishads, Puranas, mantras and other spiritual techniques.

He asserts *"The fact that I was into this family, is a validation of my belief that I was preordained to execute spiritual extension through Ayurveda by the design of destiny and not by choice of human endeavor".*

At the age of five he began formal schooling as well as a formal spiritual education. The academic journey was quite unusual but Balaji was able to reach the required milestones with ease. He was also pursuing his spiritual training alongside training in Ayurveda. On account of his focus and passion on spirituality from a very young age, he was on a different level as compared to other students. Unlike others,

Balaji always wore traditional attire. Though, it became a cause of amusement initially, Balaji had the ability to deal with this with ease and maturity. It was not easy for a young boy to be dressed differently and be spiritually aligned without becoming the butt of others jokes. He was doing this by choice and not because he was compelled to do so. It needed much more than strong will power, moral courage and perseverance to do so. Balaji won over everyone with his ever helpful attitude, co-operation and became very popular. He was also good at sports which made him more endearing. This important attribute to have the moral courage and strength to be what he wanted to be; different yet be part of the group showed the strength of his character and capacity to influence and win over people.

During his school and college days, there was a need to augment the family income and to do so, he took up the task of performing religious rituals and ceremonies at households. He was never once shy or ashamed that he was required to do things others of his age were not doing or expected to do. He also sold soap and Vaseline by walking through lanes and sitting at the market place. In doing so, he gained the unique experience of observing the behaviour and approaches of people. Hard work and discipline were already part of his culture imbibed from his father. After completing his schooling, he joined engineering. At college, he volunteered to be part of National Cadet Corps (NCC) and was extremely impressed and imbibed discipline, character and obedience. NCC made him realize the real meaning of obedience. He realized it meant obeying an order not because it is given by a senior but obeying an order because it is related to the objective of the mission to be achieved. A very important lesson which *distinguished personal obedience from mission oriented obedience.* It made him comprehend, that while personal orders could be opposed on grounds of propriety, mission based orders needed implicit acceptance. *Understanding the need of the nation or an organization as against the need of an individual.*

Learning Ayurveda

Balaji began learning Ayurveda under totally different circumstances. There were no colleges those days offering a formal structured program and a degree. Ayurveda was more or less a legacy inherited from one generation to another and was to a large extent a family endeavor. The practitioners were more like apothecaries, who learned the art of treatment from scriptures and books. They would work under guidance and acquire the knowledge through the concept of the age old Guru (teacher) – Shishya (disciple) Parampara (tradition). Balaji was pursuing these studies in Ayurveda simultaneously and would spend time with his Guru, working under him for few hours every day. He picked the art of diagnosis by observation, practical experience, discussions, dialogue and deliberations with his Guru. Significant cases were in due course given to him and he would be asked to evaluate, identify and prescribe the appropriate medicine. The Guru would keep a watchful eye to ensure the correctness of the process. Balaji learnt that Ayurveda is not just about treatment, it is much more than just providing physical relief. To him it is an extension of spiritual thinking addressing the mind of the individual to ensure more than just short term relief. It was this Guru-Shishya Parampara that excited and inspired Balaji to investigate and research in years to come and develop unique solutions to various ailments to bring succor to people not only in India but also abroad.

Exploring Avenues

After completing his studies, Balaji explored many new avenues. To him every new activity was an adventure in knowing and understanding behavior and life style. It was around early 1960's when he finished his engineering. He took up a job in Billimoria and worked for two years. During these years, his helping nature which made him popular in college assumed the nature of serving the needy. In his own way he began to do things to help those in need. This later manifested in the form of establishment of a charitable Ayurvedic Clinic in Pune, where he never charged any patient even if they were hundred of them in a day. He tried an entrepreneurial venture for sometime by establishing an Interior designing and Decoration Studio. It was during this period when he was with Interior Designing; he got to know about Rotary. As he was interested in social service and was already running a charitable clinic, he was invited to be a member. He narrates an incident "On being admitted to Rotary club, his profession was noted as Interior Design and Decoration. After a few years, he shifted fulltime to Ayurveda and healing, there was a discussion on what should be done. Balaji suggested it should remain the same as he now does *Interior Designing and Decorating of the human beings, service of the Human Body instead of the houses, Designing of human values and ethics*".

Balaji always felt that service rendered must always be without expectation of any kind of acknowledgement. He firmly believed that the good name on account of service should never be encashed for an advantage. Those were the days when communication was very difficult. There were no mobile phones and landlines were very restricted. Balaji wanted a landline connection but the process was quite time consuming. The way out was suggested by his friend that he knew a politician and he can recommend issue of phone connection on priority, if the application is made to show that it is for social service. Balaji refused because he felt exploiting the name of service to personal advantage was unethical.

On Ayurveda & Spirituality

Ayurveda is a science that facilitates increase in lifespan through application of scientific principles. It is a form of medical practice that focuses on addressing human problems at both physical and mental level. Effective practice of Ayurveda will be a combination of medicine and therapies complimented by Meditation + Spirituality + Yoga. Most commonly, Balaji feels the term is misunderstood and viewed as a religious practice. Some even consider it as an activity mired in superstitious practices. These misconceptions arise due to wrong understanding. Balaji always explains that Ayurveda is like a scientific mission intended to provide a healthy, long and fulfilling life with holistic principles which determine the course of treatment. While allopathy is concerned with problems on the physical plane, Ayurveda emphasizes the fact that the impact is much greater if the mental and spiritual planes are addressed. This is possible by a unique combination of Ayurvedic medicines and therapy on side and imbibing meditation, spirituality and yoga on the other. Spirituality is the focus on the mind above the body and it does not in any way symbolize any religious practice. Any person of any religion can be spiritual and can meditate to control the thoughts and mental faculties, achieving a positive outcome.

Balaji says that at his ashram every day before the meal a prayer is mandatory. He further explains that this is not for the sake of religion but meant to thank the creator for blessing them with food and to express gratitude. It's a symbolic tradion to bring in a semblance of discipline and create humility. He points out that every international summit in India starts with lighting of a lamp. This too, is a symbolic gesture showing the resurgence of light dispelling darkness with knowledge. He questions "Does that make this a religious practice"?

Shreeguru Balaji's mission has been to create a place where people all over the world can come and find solutions to their problems. His clinic which treated free of cost had enabled him to achieve a name to be reckoned with. The opportunity to get a large clientele of foreigners was made possible due to their infiux to Pune to visit the Rajneesh Ashram. He procured land in Karla, near Lonavla at the banks of the river Indrayani for creating an abode open to all which he aptly called "Atmasantulana" (Atma meaning soul and Santulana meaning creating harmony and tranquility). It was built to fulfill the demand of the people to be disease free i.e. to be in a healthy state of being. The aim was to create an environment in which people across the world would feel stimulated and enthused to pursue Ayurveda along with practice of Yoga and Meditation to find answers not just to their ailments but to the most persistent predicaments of the mind and heart.

It is all about faith, belief and passion and possibly some unknown force that guides Balaji to do what he has set about to achieve. His presence adds to the tranquil serenity and his words of wisdom are accepted with reverence not just because he heads the ashram but because of his credentials as a researcher, doctor and exponent of various Indian scientific methods. He believes "I have a blessing hand, which endows and enables me to give the joy and peace to others". He always attributes emotional stress to the inability of people to understand that there is no need for more inspite of having everything. The psychology of seeking "More" without realizing "why" causes unending mental trauma. He narrates a story to validate.

"One day a group of affluent business men were taken on a tour to an exemplary farm. The farm was very vast with vegetables and fruits of all kinds in abundance, that looked fresh and very attractive. The farmer was generous and as a good host asked his guests to take whatever they want. Each and every one of these businessmen went amok, unable to decide what to take and more importantly how much to take, they ended up filling umpteen bags of fruits and vegetables and carried them to their vehicle. They found that it was impossible to accommodate everything. They started to throw out from their bags. Some felt they did not need, some justified that a particular fruit/vegetable as not their favorite and some simply threw because it was more than what they actually needed". This confusion aptly describes the way we live, trying all the time to add to what we have, not realizing whether we need it or not and in the process adding to our tension and emotional stress.

Understanding to be Benign

Times are changing and so are the attitudes. Things which do not find correlation to today's thinking and lifestyle are considered to be outdated and people who believe in such things as outmoded. Every generation goes through this phase and the change being a continuous process, it has to be taken in stride. It is not how one dresses or behaves that determines what is modern; it is important to understand the relevance of an action to be judged. "I wear a tilak on my forehead, does that make outmoded? Many may think so but those who think should understand the scientific philosophy behind. The round tilak on the forehead exerts pressure on the pituitary gland thus effectively controlling the hormone development and maintaining balance." *Modernity is not opposing the legacy of tradition but accepting change. Modernity is not refusing to do but adapting to times.* Today practicing Ayurveda, yoga and meditation does involve integration of modern tools provided by science. If ancient Indian practices can adapt to the change, then why not people?

The reason Balaji attributes is lack of awareness as to the relevance and application of traditional Indian practices. Inability to understand the scientific basis behind these practices leads to viewing them as superstitions. While some practitioners may have exploited our ancient heritage to commercial advantage, that should not wish away the efficacy and reality of our traditional methods. To him, this stands as an important mission, to educate, to propagate and to penetrate.

How does this happen? He feels that it is time to introduce these practices at school level. This, he believes will achieve a twofold objective, "Firstly, it eliminates the bias regarding the common belief that it is a religious practice and secondly, learning at a young age will make them realize and understand the significance".

The example of discipline and conduct must start from home as he quotes from his personal life as an example. The attitude of rigor, self discipline, dedication and commitment to time have all been ingrained by observing and emulating his father. Today's fast paced environment must find time and space for this integration at home level.

He advocates, "Developing trust, learning to be polite, regular prayers, imbibing goodness, bowing before God and elders to inculcate humility, regular exercise of mind through study and body through sports, yoga etc, developing a contributing attitude towards the family in every possible way and finally doing whatever interests the student by doing it best. These values if inculcated will ensure a very bright future ahead".

Balaji is contented. He does not look to establish an empire of sorts. Happiness is experienced at every stage he works and he genuinely believes that he is a medium enabling changing of lives of people who seek out to him. He clearly sets an example of what he propagates "Knowing what you want and stopping when you get". To a businessman, it may seem like a lost opportunity but to a man of character and to the one with the "Blessing Hand" it's an opportunity harvested. More than 2,50,000 patients have benefited by his unique treatment, he has written more than 40 books in different languages, composed more than 20 music albums, authors the health supplement reaching more than 6 million people and offers daily TV shows on Indian philosophy and Ayurveda. For the past 40 years, he travels to Europe, four times a year offering seminars on Ayurveda, Spirituality and healing. Music Concerts, charitable trust and centres are established at Munich, Frankfurt and Gliechen in Germany. He has offered professional services in eighteen different fields including arts, cosmology, agriculture etc. In spite of all these achievements, he radiates benevolence and infuses a spirit of joy in all those who come in contact with him . He knows that being benign is not being condescending but being concerned for the feeling of others.

His pleasant demeanour, pleasing and heartening communication, concern for doing what he does with the very best of effort, humble and heartwarming nature add to the ambience of his ashram making it a true centre of learning.

For the man who says that he decided his own destiny, he has travelled a long way "Scripting the Improbable".

■ ■ ■

Key Learning Values

Understand Before Believing: Most commonly we tend to believe what others do. Judging the right or wrong and believing must be based on understanding rather than perception.

Discipline in Personal Life: This implies that one must develop a strict discipline of execution. Be it personal or professional, it is important to be oraginized in a disciplined manner. Absence of self discipline will dilute character.

Never be Biased: Beliefs like modern or outdated should not be perceptual. For that matter, no opinion should be based on preconceived bias.

Focus on Excellence: Task accomplishment is directly related to focus on excellence. Develop the habit of doing whatever one does to the best of ability.

Commitment to Quality: Quality in what we do reflects on personal and professional integrity and in a long term enables an undisputed reputation. Never compromise on quality of work or product for short term gains.

Communicate with Care: Communicating with concern, humility and informality will result in viable interaction. Communication needs to be validated by action, only then it becomes credible.

Dr. Vijay Bhatkar

Develop curiosity to know, have inquisitiveness to find out, learn beyond books, read hard play hard and be one to think first. This is the mantra to be ahead of others.

INTRIGUED BY INQUISITIVE INTRICACIES

Dr. Vijay Bhatkar

Decisive Decisions

It's always a matter of debate as to how things happen in life. Sometimes decisions define destiny and at times destiny defines itself. As one traverses the journey of life, situations compel each one of us to make choices. When such a choice results in a resounding success, it's a decision; if it fails, we attribute it to destiny. The logic behind the decision and the thought that drives the choice are often ignored and most of us quickly attribute many of our life's major twists to this word "Destiny".

To a logical mind, it's always the decision that defines what happens in future. When one finds oneself at a crossroad, unable to decide, the right choice must emerge based on analysis of facts and reason and not just emotion. May be emotion does matter but the choice must always be the one that is most logical. The mind vs heart dilemma is eternal but in the end whatever be the outcome, the factor which defines destiny is always the decision.

Vijay faced this situation twice in his life and in both cases, it's the decision that made the difference. Bright and intelligent that he was, it was not really surprising when he topped the ME in Control Systems at Baroda. For the toppers in Engineering, there was an opportunity to be directly recruited to the Post of Executive Engineer and Vijay was eligible for the same. He went through the selection process and was selected. By this time, the result for the selection for PhD at IIT Delhi was also declared and he was one of the few to be selected. On one side was the offer of a most lucrative job of Executive Engineer, which gave him a head start of over a decade by way of career and on the other was something he really wanted to do; take up research and pursue PhD and that too at the prestigious IIT Delhi. His professor's, friends and almost every one whom he consulted , advised him to take up the opportunity to become the Executive Engineer; a golden chance, they said, cannot be ignored. There was financial pressure too from the family which suited this decision. This decision could redefine his life. As always, Vijay went back to his mother, whose advice was always most valuable and most sound. He wrote to her about this dilemma and sought her views. She wrote back "The value of learning is immeasurable. Remain Hungry but study". The decision was made and he joined IIT Delhi. Years later, Vijay as the Chairman of the Board of Directors of IIT Delhi made immense contribution in increasing the infrastructure, intake capacity, research fellow intake and many others in a manner which never happened in the past five decades.

Another situation awaited him a few years later. Vijay completed his PhD at IIT Delhi. Inquisitiveness was so much a character of Vijay that his heart was onto Post Doctoral Research. He was selected for the same. Around this time, under the aegis of Dr. Homi Bhabha and Dr. Vikram Sarabhai, the Government had decided to set up an Electronic Commission with the intent of selecting a core group of scientists to evolve, develop and create a strong electronic and scientific foundation to meet future challenges for the country. Having acquired a reputation for scientific excellence, his name was suggested by IIT Delhi. Though reluctant, he appeared for the interview and was selected. Vijay was immensely impressed with Bhabha but was still indecisive because of the dilemma whether to be part of what seemed to be a government agency or be part of the stimulating intellectual post doctoral work. He fell back on his mother for advice again and this time she wrote back "In one's lifetime, there are very few opportunities to be part of an endeavor to contribute towards bringing a change in a nation's destiny. This is a national duty and hence you should never hesitate even for a second". The die was cast and Vijay joined the Electronics Commission. Down the line, he was instrumental in one of the most significant scientific contributions to India; building the fully indigenous Super computer.

Foundation of Values

It is very uncommon in pre independent India to find a family as educated and qualified as the family in which Vijay was born. His father studied at Maharaja Sayaji University, Baroda and later at Pune University. He was working as a Principal. His mother, a cultured & qualified lady, was a head Mistress of a school. Both grandparents were educated and thus the family permeated a refined ambience blending with a flavor of academics. The year was 1946 and India was at the threshold of Independence and the nation was in a grip of growing excitement and frenzy. Mahatma Gandhi to most Indians, was a god in human form and his words were treated with reverence. Mahatma believed that the future of India lay in its villages and called for the educated to migrate back to villages and assist in developing them as part of nation building. His parents were actively involved in the freedom movement and when this call came, they took it to their heart and moved back to their small village in the district of Akola. It was in this village in October of 1946, Vijay was born.

The village was no different from any other. Small in size with hardly a population of 300, no infrastructure like hospitals, schools, electrification, water supply etc. His parents went back since they decided to put in their bit to empower the people. The verandah of the Ram temple was the primary school which taught students till fourth standard. There was just one teacher but he was very committed to his work. He would teach all four standards at the same time simultaneously. Since his elder brother was in fourth, Vijay joined the same directly. Those days, there was a Taluka level examination after fourth standard and qualifying the same was essential for admission to middle school. Though, Vijay never attended the school till fourth, he passed the examination easily to be eligible for admission to middle school.

At home, it was a different picture. His grandmother would enrich them with stories. She was a teacher too. Their home had an excellent collection of books and reading was something Vijay experienced from his childhood. His parents encouraged reading beyond texts and he picked up this habit and soon was a voracious reader. His father travelled far and wide across India and would often get back with collection of books for his children which both Vijay and his brother enjoyed. The romance with reading started early which became an intrinsic quality which triggered the curiosity to know and learn. From his mother, he imbibed the importance of reading and learning, from his grandmother, he imbibed the true essence of value education through stories she shared, from his father he learnt the inquisitive nature of why? Vijay recalls his childhood experiences "I was actually lucky to be born in such an environment. My mother was a great influence and so were others. I owe it to my mother to have developed the habit of reading and importance of education. It was a childhood where I learnt so much without knowing how or feeling why? Devoid of compulsion, it just happened".

After fourth standard, Vijay had to travel to the neighbouring village for his middle school along with other children. In monsoon, they had to either wade or at times swim across the small river that flowed near the village.

This kind of a situation was prevalent across many rural areas of India. It was Swami Vivekananda who during his tour across the country observed with anguish that boys and girls had to swim across rivers to reach schools especially in monsoon, which hindered education." He said if children cannot go to school then schools must come to their door step". It is quite surprising how stories and influences of childhood come back in later years with a missionary zeal. Vijay attributes this story as the inspiration for developing the concept of "Education to Home" leveraging Information Technology in later years.

Engineering and Beyond

After completing schooling, the career options took both the brothers in different directions. He opted for engineering and his brother went in for biology. Vijay joined Regional Engineering College at Nagpur. This represented a sea change for Vijay. Coming from a protected family environment, he found himself face to face with city culture; exposure to cosmopolitan setting, interaction with students of varied social, cultural and financial background. He was also made to go through various stages of ragging. Though younger than all others, he faced these common hurdles of those times in his stride. The academic part was very invigorating, curious as he was in everything and anything, he never hesitated to ask, learn and read to find answers to his eternal query called "Why". It was during his second year, their electronics Professor, showed them a transistor radio for the first time in class and discussed the circuits in it. He would not let anyone touch it though. Highly excited and inquisitive, he found portable transistor assembly kits and set out to build a transistor. He recalls "The day I successfully managed to assemble the transistor was the day of greatest satisfaction. I was absolutely thrilled. I could tune in to All India Radio and listen to songs. I think this gave me more joy than building the super computer". This act of building a transistor entirely by himself gave him immense confidence and he began to believe more in himself.

Third year, gave him an unusual experience. Ragging was very common and many times it used to cross the boundaries of decency and get to be humiliating. This would invariably lead to tensions on the campus and many times fights between students. He was elected the President of the student Union, but there was very little he could do to stem this trend. Once the issue became so rampant that a complaint was made to the warden. The warden asked all the senior students to vacate the hostel forthwith and threatened to throw out the luggage. Since the order was not complied, he directed the junior students to pick up all our belongings and throw them onto the road from the third floor; an act the juniors did it with pleasure. To Vijay, this was not just humiliating but also made him realize the futility of ragging which people indulged purely due to sadistic pleasure which did nothing except create animosity and ruin relationship and an experience of good comradeship. During his days at Nagpur, he recollects how his family upbringing made him think differently than others. Since he never smoked, drank, dressed in fashion or was outgoing, he was made fun of by most his friends. He remained rooted to the habit of reading and learning and slowly, it began to influence his friends and they began to adapt. Vijay says "it was very easy for me to get diverted to do things most people were doing. I am of the opinion that many students do things not because they like but because they lack the strength to assert to be themselves and fear of being isolated from the group. This strength to assert oneself comes from values one imbibes at an early age".

Vijay finished his four year engineering degree in three years due to 1962 Chinese War; because of which the program was compressed to three years without reduction in syllabi. Thus, by the time he completed his engineering degree, he was hardly 19 years old. His father suggested Baroda as a choice for higher studies and in deference to his father's wishes, he joined the Masters in Engineering in Control Systems. Here, he was exposed to much more liberal and open system. The university encouraged a mingling of subjects and provided a platform for students to choose from a wide array of choices thus making the experience of education more holistic and empowering.

From Sidelines to the Ringside

Mrs. Indira Gandhi was a leader in her own right. She commanded utmost respect and not many could really find courage to face her. She was the Chairman of the Electronics Commission. She just could not fathom why India in 1980's did not have color TV transmission and she wanted to know how this could be done. Various reasons like lack of equipment, cameras, content for transmission, transmission modes, technology, administrative body etc put forth before her failed to impress her. She simply said, "It's your job to do it and just get it done", the diktat had to be executed and thus job fell on the lap of Vijay. Always up for challenge, inquisitive and intrepid, he took it up and in a short span of time created the infrastructure necessary for transmission. He focused next of creating trained manpower for manufacture and assembly of TV sets. Many factories were established especially employing women and equipment was procured and content was borrowed from Hollywood to augment the limited Indian content and the first color transmission was a reality. First, in the national capital and very soon extended to various states.

As a functionary at the Electronics Commission, he was responsible for identifying, supporting and providing resources including financial budgeting & allocation. He played a very crucial role in evolution a large number of scientific development programs.

In mid 1980's, Mrs. Gandhi's assassination brought Rajiv Gandhi to the national scene as the prime minister. Young and dynamic, Rajiv was very tech savvy and was instrumental in introducing the most important technology interventions in India, IT and Communications. To have a Prime Minister, who understood the significance of science, technology, electronics and IT was a great boon to the scientific community and Electronics Commission too was excited.

Rajiv was vigorously pursuing with USA for sharing of technology for manufacture of super computer for India especially to help forecast monsoon and predict calamities like cyclones etc. USA was reluctant to share the technology as it felt that the computing resources would be put to defence applications. Rajiv was on invitation to USA and it was expected that USA would accede to India's request with some stringent conditions. However, Rajiv's proposal was flatly refused and he felt deeply humiliated.

On return, he threw open a challenge at the meeting of Electronics Commission and asked "Is there no one here who can take this mission of making a super computer for India? The choice fell on the shoulders of Vijay. Rajiv asked him by when and at what cost, to which Vijay replied "Sir, for the cost of one super computer from USA, we will have one super computer in every state and we will require a minimum three years". Rajiv was impressed by this answer and instantly put his seal of approval and thus began the journey of innovation, invention and inspired creation.

From seemingly nothing everything needed to be created. The only time Vijay saw a super computer till then was a photograph in a scientific journal. Getting together a core team, creating a laboratory, acquiring information and knowledge, identifying suitable capacity for indigenous manufacture of electronic components etc the task was onerous. Added to it were the typical bureaucratic delays and sanctions which proved to be greater challenge. Not one to lose heart, devoting time and displaying commitment, Vijay and his team produced the Param Super Computer. But alas, India would not accept and Vijay realized that unless it gets a stamp of approval from the west the Indian diaspora will never acknowledge. In a most daring mission, he asked his team to dismantle the same and carry it in parts in suitcases to Switzerland, where the super computer was reassembled and demonstrated to the surprise of the western world. The news was out and the world's scientific community accepted this scientific miracle.

Washington Post's headlines screamed "Angry India Does It" and India did it under the leadership of Vijay. Thus, he became the architect of India's Information technology revolution and was popularly acknowledged as the "Father of Super Computer". Awards and acknowledgements came in large number. Already a Padmashree, he was also awarded a Padma Bhushan in the aftermath of this achievement. Post Creation of Param, he was also instrumental in creating the National Param Supercomputing Facility (NPSF) which has been now made available as a grid computing facility through Garuda grid on the National Knowledge Network (NKN) providing nationwide access to High Performance Computing (HPC) infrastructure. He is working on exascale supercomputing via the Capability, Capacity and Infrastructure on National Knowledge Network.

Towards the Future

The future of India to Vijay seems shining bright not because of the way economy is expected to grow, but because of the fact that India shall have the best intellectually stimulated demographic advantage of young population. The world is going through tremendous change and technology is outdated the day it is introduced. Changes and innovations are fast resulting in reduced span of effectiveness. The IT industry today has grown to be worth $100 billion in a short span of two decades. The focus is shifting to newer arenas like Nano- Bio- Info- Cognito. These and many more with greater robotisation and technology intervention in areas of human endeavor are likely to cause immense influence on how science is leveraged. Many unreal things may be real like "thought driven computers" which sense the thought and create the act, may be real tomorrow.

Will the technology take over humans? Vijay says 'The ultimate is the human brain. It links with body language, behavior, actions, emotions and gestures. No machine can ever take over as it still has to depend on the creator i.e. human brain. Technology can predict responses but cannot react to spontaneity".

To the generation of today, Vijay adds "These are the most exciting times and more challenging one's are ahead. This is the century of India and in a decade or so we will be the third largest economy in the world. The script for the real growth story has begun. Develop curiosity to know, have inquisitiveness to find out, learn beyond books, play hard, read hard and be the one to think first". For a man, who spent his life in pursuit of answers to the unknown, for someone who has spent most of his time thinking, creating and innovating, it is but natural to continue to be "Intrigued by Inquisitive Intricacies" of science in quest for a better tomorrow.

■ ■ ■

Key Learning Values

Understanding the Strength of Family Values: The significance of family values and their role in defining character is an important take away.

Learning to Self Learn: True learning is always beyond classrooms and beyond the textbooks. It is important to develop the art of reading to acquire the art of self learning.

Develop Curiosity: Knowledge can only grow if one is curious. Curiosity to know and ascertain is the key to knowing the intricacies of everything.

Identify the Passion: In life identifying what one is good at and what one can do to the best of ability is necessary to provide direction to one's life and fulfillment.

Be Inquisitive: Being inquisitive leads to discovery. To know why and find out answers to emerging challenges, the spirit of inquisitiveness is a must.

Hardwork and Commitment: Whatever be the task in hand and whatever the problems, it must be done. This approach will result in achieving near perfection and to do so, hard work and commitment are inevitable.

Strong Self Belief: New challenges can only be taken up if one has self belief. In the absence of this trait, one tends to be stuck on a beaten track.

Baba Saheb Purandare

National pride is a function of being proud of one's history. A nation without pride will always stay divided. It is time we started to "be as one, think as one, feel as one and act as one."

IN AN INFINITE HISTORICAL EXPEDITION

Babasaheb Purandare

Father's Son

The role of a father in traditional Indian households was that of an authority. As the head of the family, especially during the times when Balwant was a child, around mid 1920's, father was someone to be respected, regarded and obeyed. The interactions were fairly limited and dialogues, if any, would more or less be one sided; with father's giving out directions or opinions and the children dutifully acknowledging compliance. There was no way a child could defy or even question the decision and it was not the expectation those days to discuss and decide. It was a norm of sorts for children to look down while speaking to elders and avoid eye contact. To a growing up child of those days, a father was looked up with an aura of anxious reverence and was accorded an undisputed position of authority in the family hierarchy.

Balwant was indeed lucky. To him, his father meant the world. He was always talking, explaining, storytelling and encouraging Balwant. To a great extent, his father was responsible for triggering the historical curiosity in Balwant, by his trips to various forts and places of historical interest. Balwant recounts "I was very fortunate to have a father like him. He was a friend, philosopher, mentor and yet a disciplinarian who insisted on we children learning and understanding values and integrity". Balwant was exposed a plethora of historical trips and he clearly remembers his father carrying him on his shoulder on a Sinhaghad hike. An extremely difficult fort to climb, with steep mountain cuttings, it needed a lot of stamina. His father also introduced history to him by presenting series of books on forts and stories about Shivaji, in English and Marathi, which ignited the intense inquisitiveness in Balwant. Balwant recalls that his father was 39 years old when he was born and yet he became his father's best friend. They used to speak, chat, laugh and freely discuss a host of topics. His experiences of growing up and learning the intrigues of Maratha kingdom and the greatness of Shivaji cemented Balwant's romance with history in the years to come.

It is very interesting to realize that when most people visit forts, tombs or artifacts of historical nature, they see them as objects of relic; something of the past. His father's influence added imagination to the relics and Balwant always visualized the story behind. Seeing a fort made him imagine the glory of that time, walking on the steep slope enabled him to envision the warriors climbing the slopes and tranquil surroundings reminded of poets who wrote great poems. He developed the ability to live the history. He recalls his father with tremendous affection, respect and regard and acknowledges his mentoring as the reason for his success. He was in every way his "Father's Son", influenced and inspired by the words and deeds of his father. His father passed away in 1949; 65 years down the line, yet the painful nostalgia seems to elude the barrier of time. Such was the bond between the father and son.

Lessons Along the Way

To err may be human and to forgive divine but erring and drawing correct lessons is being a true human and never repeating is a reflection of charecter. Balwant learnt a hard lesson the hard way. In standard X, he was very weak in math's. In his examination, once, he cheated and secured 70% marks. This left his teachers and students most surprised. For someone whose marks hover around 10% or so, the jump was too substantial. The teacher smelt the rat and conducted a re-examination and Balwant was asked to solve the paper in the presence of the teacher. The result was disastrous and he got a zero. This experience taught a lesson of never having to try a short cut and there could no answer except hard work.

Balwant was a hyperactive mischievous student. He would always be up to some tricks and this would attract the teacher's attention. He remembers his strict Marathi teacher who insisted on students learning correct grammar. He was very meticulous and would go down to the minutest detail. Balwant was not so good in technical Marathi and would write in the same manner in which he spoke, which was at times was grammatically incorrect. To his teacher, this was not acceptable and he would deduct his marks. Balwant learnt from him the need to be focused in approach and doing a job with meticulous care and doing it right. The significance of perfection was driven home by his Marathi teacher.

Post schooling, he joined SP College. He was quite active in college and began to write articles in the college magazine called "Prasad". The editor of this magazine was Sonopanta Dandekar, the Principal of the college. "My articles became very popular and being the editor, he began interacting with me. He was saint of a person and was looked upon with great respect". Students in general were very fearful of him as he was the Principal. Balwant became very close to him and could interact with a lot of ease. But the mischief in him did not let him relent and one day Balwant asked him "where is your God Sir?" Dandekar looked at young Balwant and replied "As you travel to a destination, you see milestones showing Sholapur 35 Kms, Nagpur 100Kms; but for your destination to God there is no such milestone showing your distance. Your god resides in you and you have to find him". "The profound truth behind this answer" said Balwant "escaped my intelligence at that time but years later I realized the beautiful way in which he explained implying that god resides in everyone, the problem is we fail to realize and look elsewhere for everything". In addition to Prof Dandekar, there were other teachers who played a very important part in shaping the thinking and molding the character and reinforcing the self esteem, confidence and self efficacy of Balwant. It was an environment which not only fostered talent but also developed relationships between students and teachers. It was such a cohesive ambience that teachers mingled with students freely to interact and mentor. Prof Malegaonkar and Prof Sattegiri were excellent teachers, who identified the potential of Balwant as a stage artist and in a way forced him to get on the stage to act, sing or perform anything. Balwant was hesitant but on insistence took up a ten minute role and enacted the same in front of. Prof Walimbe, who was mesmerized. It was Prof Walimbe again who told Balwant that he possessed good oratory skills which lead Balwant to believe in himself and today he has delivered more than 10500 speeches on various topics keeping his audience spellbound.

The commitment, involvement and passion of his teachers at school and college was responsible for inculcation of numerous traits which became the basis for evolution of Balwant as a historian, playwright, actor, singer, painter and social worker. Balwant insists "the confidence to face the audience, courage to deal with elders and people of repute, self esteem, focus on excellence and need for perfection, integrity in thought and honest effort are the gifts from my teachers. I am indeed blessed to have learnt right way leading my life under such stalwarts".

For the Love of History

The clarion call was within and it came early. Having experienced the beauty of historical renditions as a child through the stories and trips with his father, Balwant was exposed to impressive inroads to history. It was just an unbridled passion to pursue history and study the lineage of Shivaji, his struggle, his forts and the effect on Mogul empire which became enmeshed with his interest and passion. Memories of historical stories he heard from his father from the age of four became a foundation and triggered not just an interest but an involvement that made Balwant take this as his full time occupation. On a lighter note, when people ask him about his age, he says "I am 300 years old, as my mind, soul and body is forever behind time in a magical historical world. I would say that my wife is modern and belongs to the world of today more in tune with changes of modernity". Balwant lives, breathes and visualizes history and events of the past which enable him to explain in a graphical manner to the common man in the form of drama and song. His house is no less than an historical museum having a large number of artifacts like numerous swords, a large number of pistols hanging on the alls depicting the marital status of the Marathas.

Balwant climbed almost 200 forts in Maharashtra and visited hundreds of temples. He claims even Muslim brethren may not have visited the number of Masjids, Dargas and Tombs visited by him. He did the study of all of these historical places and can tell by looking at the tombs who was buried where. "These places talk to me. I see them with different angle every time I visit them. You may have a different perspective than mine. In general, people must be visiting these Tombs and ancient places as old dilapidated structures but when I look at them, I can see, imagine and relive those bygone days and the bygone era". Balwant undertook an arduous journey on foot to Agra on the very same route actually taken by Shivaji Maharaj in 1666. This he feels was necessary for him to understand and experience the hardship in some measure. He travelled over 3 lakh kms on bicycle and an equal distance on foot to date, touring and travelling across the country visiting to understand firsthand the history and emotions of the past. "History is my life, my thirst, my hunger and my passion".

He wrote the first book at the young age of eighteen . Since then, he has written over 30 books. To name a few, "Raja Shiva Chhatrapati" and "Shelar Khinda" are most popular among the many he authored. It was Samartha Ramdass who described Shivaji Maharaj as "Yashwant (Glorious), Kirtiwanta (Famous), Samarthavanta (Capable and Courageous), Punyavanta (Righteous), and Neetivanta (Ethical) Janta Raja (People's King). This is the reason for naming his theatre act as "Janta Raja". Balwant recorded an LP (long playing) record along with Lata Mangeshkar which was named as "Shiva Kalyan Raja". The play is one of the most popular plays and has been enacted on stage for more than 1200 times, at various places Maharashtra and abroad at London, New York etc. This theatre play has been a resounding success. With over 1200 shows to its credit, Janata Raja remains an undisputed leader especially to have caught the imagination of the young and old. It is indeed commendable that Balwant makes no personal gain out of it. He created a charitable trust and the entire amount gets credited to the trust. A whooping Rs 12 Crores stand to the credit of the trust which is utilized for common good. Balwant also takes pains to explain "Most of my actors are volunteers, who wanted to part of this mission. They do it out of passion, commitment and rarely for the remuneration, which is hard to come by".

Many a times thoughts and interest gets generated but action is influenced by unknown people or incidents. Balwant was in London for three months for a study. One day he befriended a doctor by name Dr. Joseph Shaw. He was astonished to know that Dr. Joseph Shaw did his PhD., in Marathi poetry. Dr. Shaw was an expert on Sant Tukaram's poetry and a fairly conversant with Marathi. Balwant observed the British Museum Library in London had a fabulous collection of Marathi poetry. Shaw's commitment inspired Balwant and strengthened his resolve.

It is interesting to know that there was a Britisher named, James Douglas, who first mentioned about Shivaji Maharaj in 1883, in Bombay. He wrote a book on Shivaji Maharaj and the history of Maharashtra titled "Book of Bombay". It is believed that he often found it surprising and told people that there is not a single poem, book, prose, novel, drama or a history book on Shivaji Maharaj.

These incidents rankled Balwant and reinforced his determination to commit himself with more vigor and tenacity to bring Maratha history close to the people.

Indian History in Doldrums

Often it is said that a country which does not respect its history will not be respected by any. Balwant painfully observed that Indians had no such thing called the "Concept of Nation". The idea, belief and loyal submission to national citizenship in India is still missing. To some extent, Balwant feels that Britisher's gave us the feel of this concept by way of colonization which lead to national upsurge in later years for independence. He narrates two incidents: "During my stay in London. I visited a number of places; museums, libraries and historical sites. I saw a lot of statues of Kings, Queens and even military leaders but to my surprise, I did not find a single statue of Winston Churchill, the legendary Prime Minister, leader, statesman who led England in the tough times of the World War II and steered England to a victory. He was a national hero still not a single statue? I asked my friend Dr. Shaw and was surprised by his answer. He said statues are for those who need to be reminded; Churchill is in our blood and needs no reminding as he is our national icon representing everything that is British". This Balwant felt is what one means by "Concept of a Nation". "Feel as one and Be as one" and on matter of national significance "Think as One". The second incident also relates to Churchill. After the World War II, a huge public reception was organized to felicitate Winston Churchill. The venue was the famous Trafalgar Square which was packed with people charged up with emotions. People were chanting the famous poem "The charge of the Light Brigade" and were in chorus singing

"Britain will never be slaves and we shall always rule the waves". Every speaker mentioned Churchill and praised him. People were shouting" You are our Lion and we succeeded because of you". Churchill then got up and said just one line. "Now my brothers and sisters, I am not the Lion, you are the Lions and I was roaring for you". This is their national character. Balwant laments "Just look at our nation. People start criticizing each and every government that comes to power. Any one may come to power, this is democracy. The government that has been elected is mine too, this attitude is not there. I feel getting people to understand the "Concept of Nation" and devlop "National Citizenship" along with understanding History and taking pride in it is essential". National Citizenship needs pride and pride comes from feeling the glory of the past . This is the lacunae, Balwant feels he is addressing through his forays with history.

Vision Beyond

Balwant is the most revered name in Maharashtra. His contribution in making Shivaji a legend more legendary and bringing him closer to common man is beyond words to express. If one views purely from an academic point of view, he has none of the highly reckonable degrees or a PhD, yet in terms of knowledge, capacity, commitment, passion for history and the impact on society; he would indeed rank very high. He looks at himself as a student of history not an expert or an exponent. Many an awards and titles have been bestowed and yet he remains grounded and rooted to reality. Does this look like success to him? How then should one tackle to build a future where there is, as he dreams "A Concept of Nation and National Citizenship?"

Balwant has an interesting perspective on success "To me the measure of success is when "I envy no one and no one envy's me". Though I envy no one the converse unfortunately is not true and hence I feel I have a long way to go". However, he feels certain traits are essential if one has achieved some degree of recognition are necessary. He insists sincerity to one's passion, unwavering commitment. Keeping long term perspective and avoid chasing success but chasing the goal would result in achieving success. He insist the Indian concept of time management or more appropriately time mismanagement must change. Once he was asked to speak at a function in Achalpur. He arrived at the designated time and found neither the organizers nor the spectators were present. He began delivering his speech in what was mostly an empty hall. As started to saunter, they saw him speaking and wondered why the speech started? I finished my speech and concluded the session. It is not important whether anyone is present; what is important is time and that's the message he wants to give to the youth.

Value systems and family, he feels are interrelated. He feels blessed that his wife and daughter are actively engaged in social service, having absorbed the family ethos. Throughout his life, Balwant followed his family tradition of sponsoring 5 students totally free of cost for education. A practice initiated by his grandfather is still in place. At the age of 93, Balwant is bundle of energy, enthusiasm, motivation and mental strength. He still goes out participating in functions and engages himself on speaking assignments that can put people half his age to shame. He exudes positivity and an old world charm which permeates sensitivity with character. To him, the task must go on as the larger goal is to unite the nation through the medium of History. The challenge is daunting and thus his "Unending Infinite Historical Expedition" has to tread on sands of time and leaving imprints for others to emulate.

■ ■ ■

Key Learning Values

Learning From Mistakes: Everyone commits mistakes along the way. Some cover up, some blame and some learn. Best lessons are from those we learn ourselves.

Being Truthful to Self: One learns to improve only if one is truthful to oneself. Even when one has to make a choice being truthful matters.

Understanding Value of History: History is the foundation of pride. Be it national history or family history, one needs to be aware and be proud.

Maintaining Good Values of the Family: Best values are those one learns observing elders during childhood. Once imbibed, they must reinforce behav iour.

Diligence in What You Choose: Whatever one chooses to do it is diligence with which it needs to be done.

Dr. Kantilal Hastimal Sancheti

"Good work is creating a model which is affordable and accessible. good words is communicating to connect with comfort and credibility. Good deeds is ensuring services reach the underprivileged in our society".

HEALING WITH A BENIGN TOUCH

Dr. Kantilal Hastimal Sancheti

An Astonishing Windfall

It happens sometimes; not very common but not too uncommon either. At times, some gains occur in a most unexpected way from an unexpected source that too at a time when every other source seems to have dried. Kantilal Sancheti was almost at his wits end since raising funds to make his visionary project of creating an exclusive Orthopedic Specialty Hospital in Pune was getting difficult day by day. Not a man to relent, he was untiringly working on various sources for raising finances for elevating his present set up to a quality hospital. By this time, his work in orthopedics and his contribution in child care surgeries and his surgeries in rural areas for people in need were getting acknowledged. Numerous surgical health care camps in villages were becoming known to the environment.

It was not very unusual for industrial houses to donate funds for charity. One Company based at Calcutta named Bharatiya Kutller Hammer approached All India Medical Association seeking names of hospitals which are doing innovative services to meet people's needs in the field of Orthopedics and cancer, as they wished to donate Rs 50 Lakhs. The Association recommended the name of Dr. Kantial Sancheti of Pune and Tata Memorial Hospital. Kantilal wanted the donors to know about the hospital and his work before accepting their donation. Kantilal recounts "After our initial discussion, he agreed to give Rs 25 lakhs to the hospital. Overwhelmed, I thanked him profusely and told him that I would put a commemorative stone showing his name as the Principal Donor. To my surprise he said, "Doctor Saab, this money is the gift of Lord Krishna, who am I to put my name on it. It is meant for a cause and so let it be used for the cause and not for personal name". Impressed immensely as it was a very rare attribute to request anonymity especially when the donation is so staggering an amount, Kantilal made a resolve that whatever he would do, he would try to make it a legacy of the organization rather than develop a personal cult. "Our discussion continued and by the end of the meeting, the Proprietor was so impressed with my work that he decided to double his donation from Rs 25 lakhs to Rs 50 lakhs". A windfall of huge proportion fell on the lap of Kantilal from an unexpected source in an unexpected manner which helped in bringing in the desired changes.

Sitting in a simple, Spartan and yet elegant room on the ground floor of Sancheti Orthopedic Hospital, Dr K H Sancheti presides over an awesome reputation of excellence in the field of orthopedics especially in knee and hip replacement surgeries which has made orthopedics synonymous of Pune. The journey has has been long and filled with challenges and opportunities.

Invoking God's Blessing

Coming from a lower middle class family, his father was a small grain merchant. They owned a small 80 sq ft shop which was attached to their 100 sq ft home in Narayan Peth, Pune. His father, by nature was an extremely helpful person and would always take a lead in organizing and helping various activities in the grain market. Many a times, the shop was manned by his mother and assisted by the children. Though his parents were not literate from the point of formal qualification, they were highly educated. Since the shop was annexed to their home, his father expected his children to work and help in the shop. One day, Kantilal was weighing grain for a customer; he was focussing on keeping the balance exactly in the centre and in the process the tilt was slightly towards his side. Suddenly he felt a sharp tap on his wrist. His father was observing the weighing scale with equal attention; he told him "the balance is expected to tilt towards the customer and not towards you, give a little more but never little less. Remember customer is the ultimate for us and our survival lies in his happiness. It is because of him (Customer), I can provide food, clothes and a place to stay and more importantly your education". This lesson Kantilal imbibed was not about weighing more or making customer happy but understanding that treating people who deal with you with importance and enabling them to be your center of attention. This he would use in later years with great success with his patients.

The pressure on studies was not that intense and the environment in which he grew was far less study centric. Kantilal grew up working, playing and studying off and on. He was an average student and was nowhere near the category of brilliant. The idea that he would end up decades later as a doctor of such repute was not in the wildest of thoughts of Kantilal. One day, he fell seriously ill and was diagnosed with Typhoid. Those days it was a much deadlier disease with fatalities occurring at a fast pace. Kantilal was treated by Dr. Soman, his family doctor, who was a picture of dedication and patience. "Though, we could not pay his fees, he would come home regularly to treat me and assure me". This kindness and the commitment of his family Doctor impressed Kantilal and influenced him to opt for medicine as a career for future.

Getting impressed and deciding is one thing and actually getting into medical college was another; Kantilal was an average student, his performance in school did not raise an eyebrow as he was just one among the many. He was a slow learner and needed to put in more time and effort as compared to other children of his age to understand and memorize his lessons. He passed his SSC with 45% marks in the first attempt which was an achievement by itself. He managed to get admission in Fergusson College in the science stream. Kantilal was very adept towards extracurricular activities and was into these with a lot of gusto and enthusiasm. By the end of first year, the medical dream looked further as his percentage dropped from 45 to 35. He needed to focus more and work harder but was looking for inspiration and this came from his mother. She dispelled all his doubts and reinforced his self belief by telling him that "God does not send anyone to this world empty handed. He gives everyone something and you have that ability to work longer and harder; so do it". He realized that this was the only way out and set out to do it.

He decided to join hands with two of his friends, Vijay Karnik and Ashok Kukade both more intelligent and son's of doctors. The pattern for combined study they followed entailed preparing three questions each. Each would prepare answers for three and explain them to others. Thus every day they could revise 9 questions. Where the other boys studied for 4 to 5 hours, Kantilal had to put in 9 to 10 hours to cope up. Soon he was able to catch up with his friends and by the time they completed their intermediate, all three of them came out in flying colors with a first class and hence could walk in to MBBS at BJ Medical College. The turnaround happened because his mother infused a spirit of determination and joining hands with two good friends who were better than him spurred him to work more to catch up. He learnt that with effort one can make up for intelligence and collaboration must be with those who should stimulate a spirit of competitiveness.

Back to the Old Ways

Joining the medical college was an achievement and a relief for Kantilal. During the first year, Kantilal was back in his element and was fully occupied with various extracurricular activities and actively involved himself in participating and organizing various college events. As a result his performance dropped. In the second year, his father suffered from severe asthma and was admitted to Sassoon Hospital. While he was attending to is father, his friends Ashok and Vijay would take turns and sit with him and read all the lessons that were covered for his benefit. He learnt the value of relationship and true friendship which was demonstrated by his friends. Had it not been for them says Kantilal "I would have been sitting in the grain market selling grains; a very far cry from what I am today and what I actually would have been".

From his father, he acquired the nature of helping others in need. Being in medical college, he had the access to Sassoon Hospital. He would proactively lend a helping hand to any neighbor in need of medical assistance by escorting and guiding them to the hospital and enabling them to meet doctors directly. This helping nature made him quite popular and well known. In spite of his diversions, one thing he would always do was to commit adequate number of hours of study. Though not as good as a topper, Kantilal acquitted himself reasonably by passing MBBS without backlogs. Since, his marks were not adequate to secure a seat in Post Graduation directly, he had to look for work experience and this exposure gave him one of the finest experiences of his life which became a foundation for his future growth and values. It was during this time, he came in contact with eminent doctors of that time who became a beacon of guidance in the days to come.

Learning to Learn

For a young doctor in search of experience, nothing could be better than the fact that he could find employment at the clinic of Dr. E. H.

Coyaji, one of the most respected doctors in Pune. A 74 year old Parsi gentleman known for his skills and acumen, had his clinic in Pune camp. Kantilal recollects two significant experiences at that clinic. The clinic would be bustling with patients and Dr. Coyaji was always a picture of patience. It was unbelievable that on an average he used to attend to 200 patients a day. He had a system which ensured the order of precedence based on their arrival. All would be made to sit in such a fashion ensuring that the patients were seen in sequence on first come, first serve basis and not as per social status. "I was totally taken aback to see the Chairman of a major industry in Pune, Garware Ropes, waiting patiently behind his own peon. This taught me an important lesson; to treat every patient with equal importance and treat them well and secondly, I understood, people waited for him patiently because they trusted him and he invoked unequivocal faith. Something of immense significance in the medical profession". The art and science of diagnosis by examining the patient was the gift, Kantilal earned by observation One day, Dr. Coyaji called him to his room, as he entered; he saw something that amazed him. A prim elegant old doctor sitting in his chair was reading the latest edition of "Gray's Anatomy". "It was amazing to me because at the age of 74, here was a gentleman who was keenly reading the bible of anatomy demonstrating the constant need for upgrading one's knowledge to remain relevant". Kantilal realized that completing MBBS was not the end but the beginning of a life long process of "Learning to Learn".

Bombay Assignment and After

Though it was his desire, Kantilal's entry to orthopedics was more by coincidence than design. After spending a year with Dr. Coyaji, Kantilal shifted to Bombay as a Registrar of a Convalescent Home for the aged. This was a job he got on the recommendation of Dr. Coyaji and he accepted it because it was carrying the tag of a Registrar. The home had a 300 bed capacity under one single roof. At that time, Bombay was in need of an Othopedic Hospital with big capacity. The Bombay Municipal Commissioner decided that converting the convalescent home into an orthopedic hospital was more in the public interest and ordered shifting of convalescent beds to various locations in Bombay. Since he was the Registrar of the existing set up, it was decided to retain him thus he was appointed as Registrar of the orthopedic hospital. Registrar's appointment was quite prestigious and it was necessary to have at least 10 years of experience and a post graduate degree. By default, Kantilal found himself in such a position rubbing shoulders with senior Registrars though he had neither experience nor a post graduate degree.

Notwithstanding, he was not the type to be overawed. He made up for this deficiency by sheer hard work, commitment and continuous contribution. Initially, he faced a lukewarm response from his head Dr. Talwalkar who considered Kantilal as inadequately equipped for the job and one day in anger he threatened to throw Kantilal out of the window. Kantilal vowed to himself that he will get the appreciation of Dr. Talwalkar by hard work. Kantilal knew what kind of work was appreciated by Dr. Talwalkar, who by nature was very meticulous and set about to do that. Dr. Talwalkar was very particular about maintaining individual patient cards and Kantilal took up this tedious responsibility and prepared each of these cards with meticulous care and in neat hand, updating them on a daily basis by working overtime for long hours. This impressed Dr. Talwalkar so much that he accepted him as a competent doctor and mentored him.

In the later years, he would fondly refer to him as his second son, and it was Dr. Talwalkar who inaugurated his hospital at Pune. Kantilal still recollects the words spoken by Dr. Talwalkar "The Guru Dakskina (A tradition of acknowledgement in the form of reciprocity towards one's mentor) I seek is not something I want for me; I want that whatever you learnt from me and whatever you learn in life, teach it to your students" An advice, he follows like a dictum even today.

The Call of Pune

For Kantilal, Pune was his karma bhumi (Land of Destiny). Even though, he was offered a permanent post by Dr. Agarwal, Bombay Hospital trustee, Kantilal declined and opted to return to start his own practice. This he did by taking on hire the nursing home of late Dr. Motwani. It was by sheer coincidence he came in contact with the brother of Dr. Motwani in Mumbai and this paved the way for facilitating the lease agreement between Mrs. Motwani and Kantilal. It was a great risk because by this time, Kantilal had still not acquired his post graduate qualification. Alongside his private practice which picked up very well, he enrolled for his MS and completed it in due course. He was tremendously impressed by Dr. Coyaji, who was instrumental in establishing KEM Hospital and Dr. Grant, who established The Ruby Hall Clinic. It is this spirit that inspired Kantilal to dream of establishing an orthopedic hospital.

Though devoid of resources and ideas as to how to go about the same, the quest remained until one day when the answer came from the Income Tax Commissioner of Pune (his patient) who suggested to Kantilal to form a Trust. This would enable him to seek funding which had substantial tax benefits for the donors and the Trust. The first cheque of Rs 1000 was made by his mother and today the trust has a value of over Rs 50 crores. His growing reputation, acknowledgment for innovative medical services, gradual inflow of funds, the formation of a Trust; slowly lead from one to another resulting in establishment of the hospital.

Good work... Good Words & Good Deeds

For a hospital, the brand that gets recognized is the trust the doctor creates. In this context, Kantilal was a great success. All early lessons of hard work, customer centricity, commitment, learning, concern for patients, diligence and personal involvement were all put to practice. Kantilal feels that a doctor must be able to exercise more emotional influence. His presence must calm.. words must sooth and actions must reinforce. It is only then the patient feels a sense of security and confidence. His innovative thinking led to creation of artifcial knee joint to facilitate knee replacement with greater ease. His health camps for needy were greatly appreciated. His name began to be synonymous of efficiency, efficacy and excellence. "Good work" would mean providing health care in a manner it is affordable and accessible, "Good words" would signify the method of approaching the patients, hearing them out, explaining and assuring thus giving them attention not just treatment and "Good deeds" would be extending service to society at large especially to the under privileged not just by providing but involving them in the process. Kantilal believes that a person is known by what he does and good deeds are always remembered. He also adds that," Good deeds must be done not with an intention of creating a brand but should be done to bestow a distinct character". Whether it is the Chief Minister, commoner, relative, friend or a dignitary, for Kantilal every patient was equal and every one deserved equal time and importance. This approach is instrumental in getting so much respect and recognition. Awards and accolades came in plenty; International awards ranging from Harvard University to National and State level awards. The list is unending as his work was such. He displays an immense pleasure on being bestowed Padma Shri and Padma Bhushan by the President of India. He recalls "When my name was recommended for the second time, it was Prathibhatai Patil, the then President of India who mentioned that I must be given not because I contributed to medicine but because I was a good person doing good to people". Such responses says Kantilal, are the blessings that one looks for and are the best reward.

Today, his hospital is the only private hospital that has the permission to admit postgraduate students to pursue MS in Orthopedics.

Kantilal, feels immensely gratified as this gives him an opportunity to do what his Guru had sought from him as a "Guru Dakskina". Every day without fail, he starts as early as 4am; after his exercise and practice of yoga, he walks in briskly as a young man of twenties bristling with energy and enthusiasm to start his first morning lecture sharp at 6:30 a.m. Students recall that even after returning from a foreign trip and travelling by car from Mumbai, Kantilal was present sharp at 6:30 a.m. A commitment to his Guru and a commitment to his students and to himself demonstrated in action.

Introspection

No man can achieve success in any field of choice unless he has a very strong foundation of support. Support from the family, support from friends, support from all those who joined in working together in sharing his vision was key to his success. He gratefully acknowledges his wife, Anuradha, who played multiple roles to steady his family during his long journey. He was committed to building the hospital and she was committed to build him by her support. He says with gratitude visibly showing in his eyes, "She completed nursing course and worked as a nurse in this very hospital, doing everything including offering bedpan to patients in the initial stages when manpower was short. She handled our children and today, I give her all the credit for shaping their character and molding their careers. She is a pillar I rely on and the spirit behind all my achievements". He feels blessed that his children have evolved as individuals of character. Unlike him, though they were born in affluence, the home environment was spartan and was more akin to an ashram with simplicity. Children were encouraged to go to school by bus rather than by car. By grounding basic value systems, they have emerged as individuals of their own standing. His energy is effusive, enthusiasm is infectious, his motivation is inspiring and his patients trust and believe him. To what does he attribute his success; He recounts " Helpful nature and customer priority from my father, belief in hard work from his mother, treating every one with equality, continuous learning, diagnostic skills and time management from Dr. Coyaji, meticulous and faultless approach and commitment to contribute from Dr. Talwlakar, relationship and concern for sharing from his two friends and down the line need to help the underprivileged from his own background, have been instrumental in shaping my character".

To Kantilal, his dream is be recognized and remembered as a doctor, teacher and a committed citizen is far more important than his success as a medical entrepreneur. To a great extent, he feels, he has been able achieve this. What attributes does he possess which enabled him to achieve success which he would like the youngsters to imbibe? He reflects, "I feel I have always been open and ready to approach anyone for a right cause, I am a good communicator, I have been able to be one with my patients with patience, I listen to them and make them listen, creating a comfort zone with my ability to bond with people by going down at their level".

"I think it is very important not only for doctors but for every professional to make their customers feel important and for this ensuring personal touch and assigning personal time are very relevant".

Sheer contentment seems to prevail over his humble yet dignified demeanor". I am ready to die anytime; if Yama (God of Death) comes in, the only instance, I will ask for time is to let me finish the operation, if I am doing one. I wish to live after my death in the hearts of those whose lives I have touched".

With energy all pervasive and a motive to do good overpowering all actions, Dr. Kantilal Hastimal Sancheti, has still a long way to go and continue to "Heal with his benign touch".

■ ■ ■

Key Learning Values

Need for Objectivity: Be it business or personal; dealings with others must be objective and true in intention.

Sensitivity and Empathy: Professional and personal lives must have space for sensitivity towards others and empathy towards feelings.

Learning Attitude: Learning has to become a habit for life and in order to be successful, a continuous learning attitude is essential.

Sense of Purpose: A single minded pursuit of a given objective needs a strong sense of purpose. A strong commitment and faith will be essential to achieve any goal.

Listen First and Communicate Next: In all walks of life, it is necessary to develop this trait. Relationships depend on effective communication. Understanding the need and communicating will lead to long term strengthening of relationships

Dr. Shantaram Balwant Mujumdar

Hurdles are a part of life's journey. Always give it all and never give up or give in. When you give it all, new opportunities open up.

SYNERGY IN ACTION

Dr. Shantaram Balwant Mujumdar

A Resounding Lesson

It's quite strange; most unforgettable happenings are those which happen in an unexpected way, in an unexpected manner, at an unexpected moment and possibly at the behest of an unexpected person. When they do occur, they either remain a painful recollection or they leave behind a lesson which adds value to character. May be words, could be deeds, can be actions or a combination of all; put together such instances are a part and parcel of life to most but only a few draw significant lessons which transform thus making living more meaningful.

Young Shantaram was quite upset and exasperated. That day at school was not one of his good days. Boys would always be up to mischief and are handful for the teachers to control. Those were the days when the teachers would not hesitate to hand down a slap or two to discipline the errant ones and this was considered an acceptable and approved practice. Shantaram was in his element and got a tight slap from Mulla Sir for overstepping the limits of behavior in class. Though not unusual, the slap in front of the class somehow irked him. In order to get even, he thought of complaining to his father. Shantaram's father was a very influential and respected advocate in the town. By complaining, Shataram gleefully nursed the thought of putting his teacher in a tight spot as he expected his father to compel the Headmaster to reprimand the teacher for slapping him.

The office was bustling with clients and his father was animatedly explaining some points of law. Shantaram, with an aggrieved look, approached his father and complained that he was slapped by his teacher in class that day. His father looked at him and asked "Show me where he slapped you" Feeling elated that he could get his father's attention, Shantaram turned to show his right cheek. Something most unexpected happened; Out of the blue, he got a resounding slap on his left cheek. An astounded Shantaram heard his father "Never ever complain about your teacher. He is your guru; whatever he does, he does it for you".

Many years down the line, Shantaram recollects that it is not the slap but the words that resonate in his mind. Simple words and a powerful message of respecting the position of a teacher, propriety of action and understanding the limits of behavior stayed with him.

Growing Up in Gadhinglaj

Located in the erstwhile Princely State of Kolhapur, was this small town Gadhinglaj meaning Fort and the Deity. It wore a festive look that day; the excitement was palpable in the town as SSC results were out in the newspaper. In those days, hardly 20% would clear the examination in one go and Shantaram remembers that local papers prominently published the names of those who passed. It was a tradition to publicly felicitate children who passed in the first attempt. Shantaram was excited and exhilarated to be one among those to be felicitated. What was unique was the fact that the people of the town were appreciative of efforts of the children thus creating an environment of belonging and affiliation within the community.

Situated on the banks of river Hiranyakeshi, the town in 1930's was fairly small comprising of multi cultural and multi religious population. There was hardly any infrastructure to boast about; there was no electricity, only a municipal school existed and that too up to the middle school level with bare minimum facilities; teachers were paid very less salaries and the education was in vernacular language. There was no drainage or sanitation, no real health care worth a mention and diseases like typhoid and cholera and at times even bubonic plague would affect the lives of the people. Yet Gadhinglaj, had its unique character which embellished Shantaram. It was a town comprising of people of various castes, creed and religions; the community was bound together by secular outlook and life was harmonious; the only school that welcomed children from all communities and social strata and treated them equally. They were made to sit and interact with each other without any differential or partial treatment. To Shantaram, this was an experiential lesson in understanding equality of all and equality for all. Gadhinglaj gave him the "Sanskar" of understanding strength in diversity.

Prior rolthre to independence, the Princely State had banned the Congress party as the nationalistic fervour was considered anti state. Winds of change were sweeping across the country and Kolhapur was no exception; it was only a matter of time before the British would leave and very soon, the day dawned heralding a new phase for India. Post independence, India was in turmoil and Mahatma Gandhi's assassination became a catalyst for crisis for a new born nation. Shantaram was 12 years old and recalls how Gandhiji's assassination stoked first flames of intra caste feuds which led to rioting against the Brahmin community whose houses and properties were burnt resulting in migration of Brahmins to towns like Kolhapur and Pune. As a child, he understood that beneath the guise of co-existence of communities is the slender thread that binds them which breaks to chaotic situations on slightest of provocation.

Living and Learning at Kolhapur

Shantaram moved to Kolhapur in order to pursue his studies. Kolhapur those days was an education hub for the district as it attracted students from various small towns. The city had a large number of hostels, which were distinctive as they were caste centric. They admitted students based on their caste. Coming from a town which was secular in nature, this was a cultural shock for Shantaram as he was unable to understand the reason for such a caste based divisive system he was told that the Maharaja of Kolhapur came up with this idea in order to promote education and by creating caste based hostels. He thought it will persuade the traditional communities to send their children to Kolhapur for better education and prospects.

Shantaram completed his intermediate with science and nursed the ambition of becoming a doctor. Impressed by his father's oratory and communication skills the choice of pursuing law was also one of the preferred options. As his elder brother took up law and was set to take up their father's practice, Shantaram opted for medicine as alternative profession which was highly regarded as choice of the intelligent. In spite of his keenness, he could not secure a seat on merit due to a shortfall in marks.

Though not on merit, Shantaram was offered a seat on payment of donation of Rs 12000. Shantaram was thrilled as he knew that this was not a big amount for his father and he could easily pay for him. Many of his friends were in the process of taking up such seats and Shantaram was eagerly looking forward to joining them. Again the most unexpected happened which took him by surprise coupled with shock and disbelief. His father declined to pay donation for his medical seat. He told him "Son, I am willing to pay one lakh towards your education, but not a penny towards donation. Whatever you do, do it on merit and only merit will make you realize the value of it".

Hurt, distressed and disappointed, Shantaram found this argument unacceptable. He was depressed and showed his protest by abstaining from college. His mother tried to convince her husband to relent but to no avail, as he stood his principled ground. Though as a young boy, he could not see the merit of his father's decision, in later years, this incident was instrumental in Shantaram's principled stand against donations and capitation fee for seeking admissions in the institutions he would set up.

It took a few days but slowly, he accepted the reality and joined Rajaram College, one of the best for Science under Pune University. A college which encouraged high quality in teaching by accepting professors across India who were the best by providing them opportunities to stay and teach students at Kolhapur. It was here, he came across best teachers who made an impact on him. Prof Sen-Mathematics, Prof. Adhikari-English, Prof Biswas-Physics and Prof Parandekar-Botany were some outstanding teachers who made learning a pleasurable experience. It was Prof Parandekar, who made Botany, music to his ears which stimulated his curiosity to pursue M.Sc.

Getting Armed for Future

Due to centralization of Post graduate education, Shantaram moved to Pune. Armed with a letter of recommendation from Prof Parandekar, he approached the HOD (Head of the department) of Botany Department at Pune University and got admitted to the PG course. He was passionate about the subject and did exceedingly well which ultimately led him to top the university. Being a topper, he was the most eligible candidate for UGC research scholarship for pursuing PhD and his application was duly recommended and forwarded. It was up to the HOD to allot once it is approved and Shantaram had no doubts about his candidature which was purely justified on merit. In any case, he was assured of the same by his HOD.

Another shock was in the offing. He went to the railway station to see off of his HOD who was proceeding to Russia on a tour. It suddenly felt as though the platform beneath was shaking, when he heard Prof Mahabale tell him that the UGC scholarship for that year has been given to someone else. Reeling under the shock, he found it difficult to accept when he was told that the same was given to Prof Mahabale's PA. This distraught him enough to make him pack his bags and move back to his native place for some time. This experience taught him that favoritism is the bane for merit and must be resisted at all times. He came out of this crisis of denial and joined as a lecturer at Satara and a year later at Kolhapur. Having acquired the experience as a lecturer, he applied for the Post of Assistant Professor at prestigious Fergusson College, Pune and was selected. The first day was a tragedy beyond expectations. The class was huge consisting of around 175 students. Shantaram was replacing a very popular and a respected Prof VV Apte, who had a standing with the students. With his rural accent and relative inexperience, Shantaram faced a hostile reception. He was literally booed out of his class.

This was something he never experienced before and left him desperate and dis-spirited. He realized two things, firstly, he needed to be prepared thoroughly to meet the standards of his predecessor and secondly, he should try and get the class divided into two sections as teaching 175 at one go was not just challenging but quite herculean. On his request, the class was divided and by consistent efforts and hard work, Shantaram won over his students and very soon he was popular enough to attract students from other colleges who used to attend his lectures.

Moving Along the Growth Path

Steadily with passage of time came the acknowledgment as a good teacher, the doctorate and the professorship. Since he was seen as a Professor with future, the Deccan Society decided to nominate him for the election as a life member, which could eventually in due course of time would have positioned him as the Principal of Fergusson College. His election was more or less assured and there was little scope for defeat in the internal selection. He was looking ahead to be part of the Deccan Society with expectation.

A shock was in waiting as demurely as a new bride. The unwanted and the unforeseen happened and he was not elected. This was again an important juncture in his life when he came face to face with the most probable becoming improbable. This set in motion a determination to attain an important role in the field of academics. Having achieved the milestone of PhD, he became more visible in the academic circles by his publications and books. He was elected to the Senate of the University, elected as chairman of Board of Studies, Thrice elected for Chairman Academic Council. By 1973, he was a figure to reckon with and it came as no surprise when he was nominated for the position of the Vice Chancellor of Pune University. This was one role he was expecting to don with a lot of eagerness and enthusiasm. It was also a matter of pride for him because this happened purely on his merit and excellence.

Life enacts its scenes in its own characteristic way, with its twists and turns that make life a bundle of expectations and disappointments. One such scene was about to unfold and when it did, it brought another disappointment for Shantaram. All set to assume the post of Vice Chancellor, political interference ensured that at the last moment his name fell out of favor and the opportunity was lost.

"In my life, many times things that were seemingly reachable went out of reach. It is a part of destiny of denial that leads to a new destiny of success. I felt calamities became opportunities for me and series of coincidences enabled me to tackle these situations with resurgence and resilience". He says "had I been appointed to the Deccan Society, I would have ultimately become the Principal of Fergusson; had I been the Vice chancellor, I would have retired as one in due course of time; Today, I am happy to play a major role in shaping and molding education and setting new levels of excellence, something that emerged from the lost opportunities which pushed me to look elsewhere to achieve".

Philosophy Called Symbiosis

Seemingly insignificant incidents leave behind impressions spurring significant actions. At times, they become instrumental in initiating measures enabling impactful and forceful outcomes. The birth of Symbiosis too is a result of one such an incident. The year was 1969; Shantaram was the Rector of the boy's hostel at Fergusson College and was staying in the bungalow opposite the hostel. An unusual activity caught his eye. He noticed that everyday around 12 noon, a girl looking to be a foreigner would slowly sneak up to the window of a room and handover something Suspecting some unwanted activity, Shantaram sneaked into the room from back door only to be stunned. What he saw changed his thinking and personality. A Mauritian student lay on bed suffering from high fever and jaundice, the girl in question was his sister, who would come every day to give him some food as no such facility was available in the hostel. The boy got up and hugged Shantaram and cried on his shoulder and thus came out the sufferings of foreign students and their difficulties. These were especially pronounced if the students belonged to Asian and African countries and were of dark skin color. He came to know the degree of racial discrimination by the people of Pune. Through their words he realized and felt ashamed to know the reality. "People shun us, turn their backs when they see us in the morning because they think we are bad omens, refuse to rent us houses, share the seats with us in buses as they feel we are bad because we are dark. We never expected this in the land of Gandhi and Buddha; we hate to be here and look to get back as soon as we can".

Such harsh realities made Shantaram realize the need for creating an institution which offers better respect, acknowledgement, treatment and better living ambience. He took up sensitization of locals through activities in association with colleges, Lions and Rotary Clubs, articles through press, organizing activities like bringing them together with local students during Raksha Bandhan, Diwali etc.

This became the foundation of thought called "Symbiosis" A concept of "Living Together for Mutual Benefit". The basic tenet being the desire to create an organization which enables better understanding, promotes brotherhood and creates a meaningful experience for students coming from abroad. It was the dream of Shantaram to make every international student a "Cultural Ambassador" for India. He invited Mr. VP Naik, Chief Minister of Maharashtra, for an International student's function in which he made the foreign students sing the national anthem. Deeply touched by their performance the CM immediately allotted one acre of land at Senapati Bapat road where the current Symbiosis International Centre stands with pride. Shantaram needed Rs 64,000 to be paid in 10 installments to get the land and he had no money. Hearing the noble endeavor, Mr. Atur Sangatani came to him and donated Rs 5000. A letter to Mr. JRD Tata, brought in a sum of Rs 10000. Slowly but steadily the money came in from various sources and the building came up with the support of Atur Sangatani, a builder with a large heart, who never charged a fee and built at no profit basis. Thus, the Symbiosis emerged as an institution of excellence on the landscape of Pune in 1971. Since then there has been no looking back. Colleges came up one by one, from Law, arts, commerce, management, engineering and many more. Symbiosis got wings to fly with the status of Deemed University and became the first to introduce numerous courses like liberal arts. Many ministers, heads of state and ambassadors visited the campus to see its phenomenal academic infrastructure.

Good quality education, focus on merit for admissions, zero tolerance for donations and capitation, affordable learning, emphasis on quality education, pioneering efforts in innovation in education, technology infusion and learning, value education, international student hostels and cross cultural harmony have remained steadfast areas of emphasis for Shantaram. Early lessons in life and the experiences he acquired left a mark which reinforced his commitment to ensure a high integrity in standards set for the institution. In spite of his achievements and numerous awards like Maharashtra Gaurav, Punya Bhushan and the prestigious Padmashree and Padmabhushan, he remains rooted in simplicity. Simplicity is not just a physical manifestation but one which is visible in expression, feeling and behavior. He believes education is future and India must educate. He also strongly advocates that only private education that can do justice in enabling excellence with equity and expansion. The present license raj in education must be put to rest to ensure faster access to affordable with acceptable quality. As he looks ahead, one does not see an iota of stress or even a slight sign of fatigue. His agility, energy and enthusiasm belies his age. His humility and simplicity wins over all those who interact. Despite of being the Chancellor of Symbiosis International University, he still remains at heart a Professor, teacher and a mentor who understands that the foundation of life and living in any society rests with those who educate. To him, the task has just begun and he looks at the road ahead with a renewed vigor. He still needs to persevere, still needs to focus and he still needs to be a symbol of "Synergy in Action" to set the tone for future and inspire many to seek new challenges and succeed.

■ ■ ■

Key Learning Values

Hurdles are Part of Life: Journey of life will have its share of hurdles and these need to be addressed. Never to give up or give in approach will always assist in shaping better future.

Treat Difficulties as Opportunities: Every time one faces a set back, look for an opportunity. There is always a way if you look for one.

Importance of Values: There are always easier options if one adopts actions that are not value based. Though choosing value based actions are difficult, in the long run they always pay.

Identifying A Reason for Living: It is important to identify one's reason for living or a mission to live for. This provides direction and courage to achieve the same.

Persistence and Tenacity: Once an objective has been set, there cannot be two ways. The effort must be persistent and with tenacity or else the objective remains a day dream.

Empathy in Action: One's experiences in life must lead to empathy in action for others benefit. If one can do so, effort must be made to give what one could not achieve to others by enabling and supporting them. "What I could not do, I will do for others" should be the motto.

About the Author

 Prof (Col) N Ram Gopal served in the Indian Army for three decades in India and abroad with distinction on all operational areas.

He is a Post Graduate in Management from Pune University, has completed "One year Executive Program in Leading and Management" from IIM Calcutta. In addition, he holds Post Graduate Diploma's in Management (HR&PM) and International Humanitarian Laws. He also holds "Train the Trainers" Certification from Rutgers State University, New Jersey and is qualified in Level I Participant Learning Methodology conducted by Harvard Business School in Association with Harvard Publishing.

Post his Army career, he was Associate Director and Professor with MIT School of Business Pune till Dec 2014. Presently, he is an Adjunct Professor at IBS Pune teaching a wide range of subjects such as Marketing, HR, General Management, Ethics, Corporate Governance and Communications.

He is recognized as "Paul Harris Fellow" by Rotary International USA and was bestowed "Best Teacher Award 2012" by Maharashtra Academy of Engineering Education and Research - World Peace Centre (UNESCO Chair) in 2012.

"Defying Destiny" is his maiden venture as an author.

He currently lives in Pune with his family and enjoys winter mornings in the sun with his Labrador. He can be contacted on email at rgopal44@yahoo.com.

www.ingramcontent.com/pod-product-compliance
Lightning Source LLC
Chambersburg PA
CBHW030413020726
47493CB00003B/1047